MR. SOMEBODY SERIES

THE CRYSTAL GATE

By

MATTHEW LECHER

About the Book

The Crystal Gate brings the cold hard truths of what families endure do to drug addiction. One in every family is affected by drugs. A page turner of real situations that become all to familiar to the addicted. A riveting tale finding hope when all else seemed lost.

About the Author

Matthew Lecher grew up on the streets of Milwaukee Wisconsin. After many years and losses due to drug addiction still resides in his home state of Wisconsin.

Dedicated to

Dennis and Nancy for keeping their promise.

Table of content

CHAPTER 01   14

    "Reality is an illusion, although a persistent one."   14

    –Albert Einstein   14

Chapter 02   27

    "There is always some madness in love, but there is always also some method in madness."   27

    -Friedrich Nietzsche   27

Chapter 03   37

    "Men are not gentle, friendly creatures, wishing for love, which simply defend themselves if attacked...A powerful desire for aggression has to be reckoned, as part of their endowment."   37

    -Sigmund Freud   37

Chapter 04   39

    "Unfortunately, there is no doubt, about the fact, that, man is, as a whole, less good as he imagines himself or wants to be. Everyone carries a shadow, and the less it is embodied, in the individual's conscience life, the blacker, the denser, it is."   39

    -Carl Jung   39

Chapter 05   42

    "The greater the power, the greater the abuse."   42

    -Edmund Burke   42

Chapter 6   47

    "All the world is a stage. All the men and women merely
players. They have their exits and their entrances.And one man,
in his time, plays many parts."   47

    -William Shakespeare   47

Chapter 07   54

    "Each relationship strengthens a character in you."   54

    -M. Merdok   54

Chapter 08   59

    "He who has a why to live, can bear with almost any how."   59

    -Friedrich Nietzsche   59

Chapter 09   64

    "Then he can worship and be enlarged by his worship, for he
can never go beyond this sentiment."   64

    --Ralph Waldo Emerson   64

Chapter 10   71

    "It doesn't take a lot of strength to let go. It takes a lot of
strength to hang on."   71

    -J.C.Watts   71

Chapter 11   78

    "We are made wise by the recollection of our past"   78

    -George Earl Shaw   78

Chapter 12   80

"Man, never so often deceived, still watches for the arrival of
the brother, who can hold him steady to a truth, until he can
make it his own."   80

-Ralph Waldo Emerson   80

Chapter 13   83

"They wish to be saved from the mischief of their vices, but not
from their vices."   83

-Ralph Waldo Emerson   83

Chapter 14   86

"Always kiss your child, even if they are asleep."   86

-Ace Jackson Brown Jr.   86

Chapter 15   93

"Being able to accustom ourselves to some degree of physical
pain, without immediately reaching for something to dull it, is
an important life skill."   93

--Robert Greene   93

Chapter 16   96

"The longing to commit madness stays with us throughout our
lives. How is it that we hurt those we love, although we know
remorse will follow? Our whole being is nothing but a fight
against the dark forces within ourselves. To live is to war with
the trolls in heart and soul. To write is to set in judgment of
oneself."   96

--Henrik Ibsen   96

Chapter 17   101

"Each night, we die a little death. So why do you continue to carry your woes? Awaken reborn."   101

--M. Lecher   101

Chapter 18   104

"Pain is also a joy. Curse is also a blessing. Night is also a sun. Go away or you will learn that sage is also a fool."   104

--Friedrich Nietzsche   104

Chapter 19   108

"At the most we can do is make hysterical, unhappy people normally happy. We bring them back to the normally unhappy."   108

--Sigmund Freud   108

Chapter 20   118

"I wonder if this is how the Lord feels, able to see what foolishness men are up to, but canna do a bloody thing about it."   118

--Diana Gabaldon   118

Chapter 21   120

"O' while you live, tell the truth and shame the Devil."   120

--William Shakespeare   120

Chapter 22   127

"Speak of progress as much as you want. Even when you take out the canines of a tiger and he can only eat gruel, his heart remains that of a carnivore."   127

--Gustave Flaubert   127

Chapter 23   131

"Men will only become better when you make him see what he is like."   131

--Anton Chekhov   131

Chapter 24   137

"The truth is always pure but never simple."   137

--Oscar Wilde   137

Chapter 25   140

"When sorrows come they come not as single spies, but as battalions."   140

--William Shakespeare   140

Chapter 26   142

"The course of true love never did run smooth."   142

--William Shakespeare   142

Chapter 27   148

"Love, friendship, respect do not unite people As much as a common hatred for something."   148

--Anton Chekhov   148

Chapter 28   152

    "The whole law of human existence consists in nothing other
    than a man's always being able to bow before the
    immeasurably great."   152

    --Fyodor Dostoyevsky   152

Chapter 29   157

    "Since everything in nature answers to a moral power, if any
    phenomenon remains brute and dark, it is that the
    corresponding faculty in the observer is not yet active."   157

    --Ralph Waldo Emerson   157

Chapter 30   164

    "I will show you fear in a handful of dust"   164

    --T.S. Elliot   164

Chapter 31   171

    "Brothers and sisters are closer than hands and feet"   171

    --A Byzantine Proverb   171

Chapter 32   177

    "A little poison, now and then, maketh pleasant dreams and
    much poisons a last for a pleasant death."   177

    --Friedrich Nietzsche   177

Chapter 33   182

"The safest road to hell is the gradual one- the gentle slope, soft underfoot, without turnings, without milestones, without sign posts."   182

--C.S. Lewis   182

Chapter 34   190

"Forgiveness does not change the past; it lays siege to the future."   190

--Paul Housa   190

Chapter 35   205

"The only source of knowledge is experience"   205

-- Albert Einstein   205

Chapter 36   210

"I form the light, and create darkness: I make peace and create evil, I the lord doeth all these things."   210

-- Isaiah 45:7   210

Chapter 37   216

"It is not I who created myself, rather I happened to myself."216

-- CJ Jung   216

Chapter 38   228

Chapter 39   229

Chapter 40   235

Chapter 41   243

"Find a job you love and you will never work a day in your life"243

Mark Twain   243

Chapter 42   247

"In the beginning was the Word, and the Word was with God
and the Word was God"   247

--- John 1:1   247

Chapter 43   253

Chapter 44   255

"Great and marvelous are thy works, O Lord God the Almighty"255

Revelations 15:3   255

CHAPTER 01

"Reality is an illusion, although a persistent one."

–Albert Einstein

It was an April evening. It was warm enough to have the windows cranked down. The cool breeze washed over my face; it was refreshing.

I was tired. My senses peaked but dull. The days had run into a timeless panoramic view. My body was demanding many needed hours of recuperation, rest, food and a quiet atmosphere. I knew that without my conscious allowance, my body demanded retreat. Before the blackness, that began shading my vision and enveloping me, I had to get away, away from the evil of man's mind.

I had just left by sneaking out of that very odd couple's house. Was that full grown man have on a woman's night gown? Yellow long and billowing with a wide man's berth, my god, he was wearing it! I guess I shouldn't judge, I am probably thought strange to some. There are all kinds and all walks of life. I care nor dare to dream what he thought seductive.

I had left without notice. I could hear her advances. She laughed and giggled.

I had to leave! I had to vacate. It was better to leave and get home with my wallet yet intact. A con will always strike when your weak, sleeping, or in a psychotic state, which I have begun to have many.

On an old country road, I maneuvered the domestic, soccer mom's van at a speed that felt adequate for the mood I was in. It was a thrill to push the gas pedal, increase the speed, and embrace my plan that the rest of the night would be mine. Or so I thought.

Coming upon the village, it would seem to all appearances to be a quite normal evening. The roads were empty and the flooding from the recent storms had receded.

I stopped at the stop sign and as my blinker ticked on, I took a left. I barreled round the curve advancing me towards my next turn onto Karl Street. I signaled my turn and made another left. My house would be three houses in from the corner. I could see the porch light illuminating the driveway.

I pulled into my lot and hit the brakes. The front end squeaked a bit, for I had recently installed new brakes and an outer tie rod end. It hadn't quite broken in yet. I put the van in park and using the side rear view mirrors checked to be sure I had pulled in enough not to have the tail end in the road.

A vehicle that resembled a jeep caught my attention, pulled up at the end of the driveway and extinguished the headlights. My adrenalin surged. Who would be visiting at this hour without calling first? I sure wasn't expecting company. The only other explanation would be to consider it was the Sheriff's department.

I had a past with the department ever since I moved into this god forsaken county when I was hassled and pulled over almost a year ago. That situation had landed me in jail. I had been arrested for drunk driving leaving my house that evening. I assume in small towns the boredom gives them cause to run the vehicle plates and just wait to pull you over when given the chance. This was much like cat and mouse or the loving house pet that bolts out the yard after the rabbit.

I must inform you, I surely don't make a habit of this behavior, but this incurrence, I was, as many to understand, was Dirty. My pocket laden with a prescription bottle with individual pre-weighted tiny zip sealed baggies of meth amphetamines. And yes, to answer that electrical static impulse that just buzzed up that wonder, I was a dispenser of sorts, and was known that it was probable that I may have enough drugs on hand to share. There was a water pipe in the passenger side, captain's chair coated with enough residue of the illegal drug, alone worthy of a felony arrest, and let's not forget the scale that happened to be in my lap.

I knew the risk of possession of the drug and its paraphernalia was a sure trip to prison. I was already on parole for a prior drug charge of the same drug I was at this moment in possession of.

Panic came over my senses seeming obstruct my air supply. Like a computer program my mind raced through the legal aspects and ramifications implemented. If I could only control the course of the event which was about to ensue; therefore, I may be able to control my very near future and my plan unfolded.

Get out the car, run for the house, and do it fast, was all I could think.

I opened the van door, smoothly and with the flick of the wrist, I tossed the water pipe under the vehicle. I stepped out and swinging around the vehicle door, gave it a good push which closed the door with a bit of a slam. My step was from 1 to 60, at least in my mind flooded with adrenaline; it was no holds barred. My whole intent was to be in that house 2 minutes ago!

It wouldn't be fair of me not to describe the scene and what a scene it was! I am barefooted with a flannel housecoat on. My pants were sagging from the hips from emaciation and limiting my range of motion. I was without a shirt, bare-chested and boldly tattooed.

If I could only make it to the door! If I could get inside the house; he surely won't chase after me! As I made this great show of record attempting to elude, I spilled my keys from my pocket. Damn, there are six of them!

I looked back! Never look back. I should have learned that from Sunday school when Lot's wife looked back as God destroyed Sodom and Gomorrah, she was turned to salt! And what did I do? I looked back.

Well, I better fill you in. A couple of months ago I had been walking the streets and was happened upon by a sheriff. The same sheriff, mind you, that arrested me for drunk driving. At this juncture, I had been, coming from an associate's home, walking a lawn mower to be used the following morning. When I walked past his parked vehicle he exited the vehicle and stopped me.

I had come from a big city to his county, and the officer knows me by my driving and criminal record. In the rural towns, the law enforcement somehow believe, it is their duty to keep track of the new- comer. Anyways, the officer, knowing I was on parole, made the assumption I was intoxicated and at that juncture, thought to take me to jail. I was intoxicated, and pushing a lawnmower at odd hours of the night is suspect. I never made it home to my wife that night.

So now you have the complete history of me knowing and interaction with the sheriff named Joe.

So where we ...oh...   trying like hell to get inside the house.

I made a beeline to the door. I found the key I needed, because I had color-coded sheaths for each key. I fingered the key into the lock. The key slid home.

No sooner than that, I heard a tussling and exactly what I was trying to flee. "Sir, Sir, Sheriff's, department, Oh Matthew. I thought u were Kim" he badgered and cut the distance in a stride. He was at my tail coat and I knew the voice. It was Joe the k-9 cop.

I had to acknowledge. Maybe I shouldn't have. But I couldn't play deaf. He knew me!

"Oh, it's you. You scared me," I replied.

"Where is Kim?" he asked.

I knew he was using her as an excuse for him to investigate my mindset, but I was already shaking like a queer at a hot dog stand. It was obvious that I was nervous.

"Kim is wanted because she has a warrant for her arrest," Officer Joe proceeded to inform me.

"Oh she's around somewhere. I was looking for her myself," I rebutted. "We weren't seeing eye to eye, so she apparently took a walk.   "I had gone for a drive to find her; I am not expecting her back any time soon. We don't see eye to eye all that often," I stammered.

The situation had my nerves frayed as if they hadn't been before this ordeal. Damn it, I told myself. Get control of yourself!

"Have you been drinking?" This was Joe trying to find, the in, to harass me further.

"Hours ago I had a shot or two, too long to become an issue, Joe." I fired back.

I couldn't evade the fact that I needed to get away, get clear of this nosey cop. The danger I was now face to face with equaled to a lengthy stay in the upstate penitentiary.

Now I can surely hear Charlie, my Brother Randy's dog, yipping' away on the other side of the door. Charlie was what I call a rescue dog. You see, my older brother Randy, dated, let's just say, a woman with issues. The issue at stake being, she tied cute little Charlie to the toilet with a chain of only three feet. Charlie was rescued, by my big brother Randy, for the lead role as mascot for Randy's landscape business. Charlie definitely has his own personality and completely loveable except when he got mad, but, most often, he was loveable chasing butterflies. Sometimes ,you may find irritation at having to go find him after chasing rabbits and squirrels; and be sure not to leave out ,for God knows why, Charlie would find other animal feces to roll in before wandering back to the house reeking to high heavens like feces.

Now I have to paint the emotional value when it comes to Charlie for you to feel the gravity of the situation. As the landscape company mascot, any given day, in the warmth, of basking in the sun, you would find Charlie's head out the passenger's side window of the dump truck, long ears just flappin' away in the wind, while sitting on my lap, bouncing down the road. Charlie, you may as well say had luck on his side; for when taken on a job cutting up firewood on a customer's land, there was an accident. My brother Randy decided to move his dually tired mammoth of a truck. Well Charlie must have believed he was going to miss something for he sure tried to jump into the open door of the truck at the same time Rand hit the gas. Charlie landed under the truck as the double rear wheels then rolled over his little body. Randy thinking to put little Charlie out of his misery took off down the driveway to the barn. Instead of returning to the scene with the gun from the barn for situations like this, Randy came back with a mall type hammer. Randy's face read pain with the thought to put poor Charlie out of his misery with punishing blows to the head. The only words he said were, "I couldn't find the bullets."

To make this short as possible I talked Randy to see what the veterinarian might think. Charlie ended up with his jaw wired and then plastered with almost a full body cast this being after a long surgery stopping the internal damage. The time invested in the care of this rescue dog, needless to say captured the heart.

Now that the picture painted, we can get back to that cop, Joe. Now Joe was probably a soldier before becoming a cop. At least that's the swagger he displays. He's mean, the bully type. I sure don't care for bullies.

"Where else are you coming from?" Joe began to drill.

"I was in pursuit of Kim, but she went off with the neighbor, Steve," I said without missing a beat.

The thought of the next years without privacy, let alone, no access to the woman, obviously needed for the benefits, with flight forefront on my mind, I nervously turned the key as the tumblers found home.

Now I may be a little fuzzy on the specifics, but I leaned in on the door. What was I thinking! He said "Stop!" I looked at that, like stopping in the middle of a yellow light, with a car at full speed, coming up fast. Everything inside me said, "Go!" So I went.

The officer attempted to grab me as I crossed the threshold of my private comfy little home. He missed and I swung with agility I know not where from. I was trying to bar his entrance with my body weight against the door.

This meant war! Whatever I had planned next, I will never know because there was no plan at this stage in the game, silly. As I think back on the whole situation, I have to believe that, as the dominoes began to fall, Officer Joe had thought a couple steps ahead. While I thought I was winning with high hopes of eluding this cop; he had fully intended to grant me access to the house. Then, technically, he could legally search the residence according to some jumbo ACT 79. Knowing, I was already on parole and given to suspicion, the law allows law enforcement access to a residence of any felon who is still under the supervision of the State by the Department Of Corrections. I fell under that mess, and I fell into his trap.

So here I am breaking access to the house and in that same moment, doing my damn best to isolate myself from Joe. As he pushed and I pushed; for the door was in between us, and I managed to vacate the flannel housecoat I had been wearing. In its pocket was the prescription bottle laden with pre weighted little zip lock baggies of crystalline substance. My concern was to banish its existence or try to remove it from my person.

Well Officer Joe did manifest his wish; for he came crashing through that flimsy door. He surely used all his might. When his shoulder hit that door after a time or two, it sure knocked me into my kitchen table located behind me.

Joe grabbed me, but I wasn't ready or willing at that moment to give him any such courtesy, when to all appearances, I had to believe he had just become the bully from my junior high. Well I pushed. He shoved. I swung and he ducked; and I to this day cannot tell you the reasoning that I was using in such a handicap mentality. Somehow we ended up on the kitchen floor. It was a fight!

So now little Charlie is yapping. I'm sure Charlie didn't know quite what to do. By the way, he hates wrestling or violence of any kind, let alone, his keeper under attack. By now, Joe and I are truly making a mess out of my kitchen. It wasn't looking good, as we, no holds barred, were entangled in what seemed a struggle for life itself. I see Charlie in and out of my line of sight. I wasn't so sure if poor Charlie would indeed bite Officer Joe. He's jumping and nipping. All I could think is He sure is a loyal dog. If Charlie had been a pit bull old Joe would have had to come back another day.

You see now the thing with crystal meth is that though you become emaciated for lack of nutrition and the lack of rest, you can ring that bell to the tune of David Banner and the great green hulk! With the strength of four men, although strangled for space due also to fact old officer Joe is putting the wrestle moves on me. Joe was tirelessly trying to restrain me. I simply pushed up off the floor. Now as the strength brought Joe and I to my feet, face to face still in that wrestle hold.

I could no longer hold my laughter at the gravity of the situation. I think this really bothered Joe. Whether it was Joe who kicked off the cabinets firing us back out the house door, I don't know but now we landed in the grass outside the house. With me still finding humor in an altercation with my nemesis; I came full circle and it sunk in that this was surely not going to end any better. I was screwed. I felt the ice of the cold steel clamp upon my wrist and the riveting sound as the handcuff tightened with climbing pressure.

Of course, in Joe's victory, his dance made me want to vomit as he began his rummaging through my home; and I, obviously, had to view this unable to protest, not for lack of trying.

Joe went straight to my bedroom as I stood pretty much in shock at the whole conundrum that had befell me. Although handcuffed and butt hurt at the situation I was in, I happened to look down; and, as sure as shit stinks, there, at my feet, was the prescription bottle with the multiple pre-weighed, small, zip lock packages of that crystalline substance.

Just then my friend Nick came barreling through the door. Now I rent Nick the basement of my home. I met Nick at another incarceration, several months previous. Nick is an alcoholic and had bailed out of jail, on criminal charges for drunk driving. Nick had lost his residence and I allowed him to stay with me. So I imagine, hearing the commotion, he came up to see what kind of shape I was in; or to be sure I was alright. I could plainly see he was hammered. I had no doubt for there was always a habitual daily dose of vodka; for Nick had turned me on to the good stuff being, at least, eight times distilled for a better quality beverage.

By knowing the legal ramifications of police policy if discovered that Nick being out on bail, this was a definite violation of his bond. All it took was for me to show him my new jewelry and I saw the recognition in his eyes. He appeared to have turned sober in that instant. I, certainly was praying for a reprieve, hoping Nick would have scruples enough to vacate with that prescription bottle twisting around on the kitchen floor directly in front of him; but Nick fled back out the door he had originally entered through. The only access to the basement was from a cellar door outside the house. Nick staggered out the kitchen door allowing the screen door to slam.

Joe, who must have come out of his "zone" from his search, obviously, deciding it to be his job to police my home, now giving chase after Nick. I imagine the sobering idea of the travesty impending had dawned on Nick and given him the gumption and agility to keep about ten feet in front of Joe. I could almost see Nick, who made it to his room through the cyclone door without incident, was most likely piling the washer and dragging the dryer to blockage the entrance. Joe kicked against the door to no avail and for a second attempt the search resumed.

He, again, passes by the bottle of crystal without notice and it lay a foot from the garbage can. This search forged on for a better part of an hour before my

Upon reaching the county jail, the deputy's received me. Knowing me from my last couple stays, they treated me like a runaway child coming back to the safety of home. The regular question and answer session quickly frays my last nerve and, finally, off to the detox cell I go.

The next couple of days are hardly worth memorable. I guess I hadn't been real clear on the question and answer session informing them of the hell from withdrawal, I was sure to encounter. "How long have you been using?" the deputy had asked if I remember right. Loaded question like that deserved no answer. How much of what and exactly how long has it been since I left here? Is what I should have said, but I had vaguely recalled the darkness wrap its warm comfort around me. I remember dripping sweat on some wakeful moment. A blood pressure check, mumbling from the end of a tunnel, engulfed again in blackness.

A nurse woke me holding me head up forcing me to drink water. Yeah, these small town jails, you never get this treatment of care and concern in the big city. I recall a calm voice, "Take this Matt, you will get through this." She had given me a pill and monitored me as I swallowed a little water from the cup given to me. I recall shaking uncontrollably. I was also soaked to the bone as if someone had dumped a couple gallons of water on me.

I knew I had put a hurt in' on my body. It was started with only a couple days until it escalated to weeks then months. It was time to pay the reaper. The weeks without sleep and forcing food down my throat. You realize a lot when you eat a cheeseburger and it gives you the feeling as if you had just digested a Valium. When you urinate because you finally remembered you had been on your way to the bathroom but got sidetracked; and the smell of your urine is so terrible your gag reflex kicks in. Beer is all you have been drinking and you realize your piss smells like a porta potty often found at the carnival reeking in the eighty five degree heat. I had sure been enjoying cool alcoholic drinks on a regular basis since I could remember. I really wasn't a big drinker but my roommate, Nick had kept the house stocked with beer and quality vodka always within reach.

I don't know how long I was in that cell, but from a regular visit from the deputies and nursing staff, I had acquired an arsenal of powder packets of juice mix in attempt to hydrate myself. Everything about living had to be put on auto pilot. The only time I stayed conscious was long enough to have the luxury of a shower. Soon you start to realize, as it dawns on you, you have managed to have dug yourself one hell of a deep hole and to be sure the parole agent was filling that hole with you in it. Your body slowly returns to the twitches and habits you can only associate to when you're incarcerated. You reflect back and ask yourself," how did this happen?" Living in the country my life had inevitably returned to what I had been trying to elude in the city. To figure it out I had to go back to an earlier release as there have been quite a few.

Chapter 02

"There is always some madness in love, but there is always also some method in madness."

-Friedrich Nietzsche

14 years ago

Released from a minimum security prison, the electronic GPS bracelet is finally being cut from my ankle. The last year I have been on work release, but having to yet return the security of the prison for sleep. Let us not forget the weekends for I was still to endure the meals consisting of processed food which still makes me shutter. I had saved a good amount of money, especially for being incarcerated. No qualms there!

My loving sister Julie had previously helped in viewing several apartments that fit my budget. Her better judgment in use, she decided on a one bedroom quite close to the independent living placement my dear grandmother was residing in. It was about a half a mile from Julie's home, where she resided with her husband Brian and the three adolescent children.

The much sought after apartment would not be available for me to move into until the first of the month. Unfortunately, the state correctional prison institutions are not permitted for sanctuary. After a period of incarceration, one is often become reliant on the structure that supplied shelter and meals. When your time to go is upon you, you must leave. My sister Julie and her husband decided to let me, literally, camp out in their two acre backyard. A camping tent was erected near a fire pit I am sure was used for family time of their own; and I would be needing to use in order to sub-due the cold darkness of the October night. Fortunately Julie's husband worked in the same town that was home to factory job that I had been employed at while working at while at the prior residence of the institution. My brother in law made sure to get me to work on time; I am sure hoping I continue to live in a responsible fashion.

As I think back on the situation of those living arrangements, I have to chuckle to myself wondering what was exactly thought of me that my brother in law was adamant that I not be given access to their residence accept to get ready for work each morning. Speculating, maybe the belief that family was doing their due diligence and protecting the kids from my influence or wild ways?

One night it had rained quite heavy. Those drops from heaven accumulated into a torrential downpour. I slept on an air mattress elevated from the ground. My small thirteen inch television, remnants of my incarceration, was powered from an extremely long extension cord snaking away from the house, to the low spot of the acreage, the fire pit. I was in hazard of electrocution or at least a serious wake up call. If the water were to connect those leads, water and electricity can be quite lethal. So as I am, surely, passed out from watching that camp fire half the night, not to mention, those twelve hour work days. I was awakened to the shaking of the tent by my sister. My alarm clock read 5:02. Well as I gathered my wits, it dawned on me maybe my darling sis felt bad since it was especially cold and had a change of heart and chose to allow me a night in the warmth of the house with a shingled roof in company of my dear nephew and nieces. No, they let me slide in from the rain, but only for that morning.

I often pondered, what was really thought of me? Obviously, I had been in prison, or was it because of the past drug use, that I was in some way, surely not to be trusted? Had I actually been put in the collective of the prison population which includes murders, rapists or worse yet a pedophile? In all honesty I don't fault the guy. I know that his abilities are only applicable in his world of labels, sciences, and mechanics of his profession.

I was overfilled with bubbly, for after my address was actually finalized and come to fruition, my sister's family helped me move in my new abode. I, then, could only find humor in my brother in laws best attempt to aware me with the warning in such a speech as this:" If for any reason, or, at any time, do my children come to your door, you are, immediately, to turn them away ; or I will..." The terminology evades me, but something to the effect of beat me up or kill me. I believe for validation he ended the remark with, "Am I clear?"

Again I have to ask myself, am I to be offended? Of course not, for I can only ascertain that in some remote fashion, he was only trying to shield his beloved family from the woes of the world that he by interpretation perceived I represented. I had to take into consideration, for my own mental stability, due to his inadequate sense, or ignorance, of my reality, he was convinced that I would or could cause harm. My mind soared for I could only perceive my own thoughts that maybe he was under the impression that I sold drugs to children, for there are many that do, to enhance their own wishes and fill their pockets with greed money. And I understand in a sociological view and of the world view on the drug trade. To be clear, I definitively would have no hand in that atrocity. I had to release that moment of emotion as best described as a dandelion blown to seed.

On the flip side of the coin, I have to be quite appreciative, in the highest regards, for the family help offered in establishing a dwelling to live in; and the help in accumulating the comforts of what makes an address a home. My apartment had very little use other than sleep. I was working six days a week, anywhere from twelve to sixteen hours a day.

Trying to maintain structure, as in the prison setting, is comparable to a birds wings clipped. Well those wings grow back after the release. Of course for a couple weeks, I was part of society.

I was soon in touch with Theresa, whom, herself had recently been released from state custody none too soon. Theresa, herself, a woman and keen to the art of persuasion, found herself in my company on evenings after I returned from work; or, obviously, my days off were fair game.

There was the much desired relationship with my son Matthew coming to fruition, as I was permitted his attendance on days off. I cannot take credit for being a very decent father, for selfish means of drug addiction kept me unstable, unreliable, and certainly not often sober. Matthews's younger years, due to my own neglect, visits weren't as often as should have been. Visits to an institution, the penitentiary, were sporadic at best. There were times, when I would crawl out from under some rock, and take heed to the idea, I knew well enough, a child needs a father and a father's love, and in my mind I was doing what I was capable of. I fret to say that Matthew only received a skeletal relationship with me, his biological father. The well-meaning adaptation of the concept to raise Matthew according to the principles and virtues that I, obviously, was not so great at; truth be told, I still gave it my best shot. In so much, I wasn't so great for the task.

So as I was newly released from the structure of our penal system, trying my best to function on my own accord. I decided to buy a car from an old acquaintance so I could manage transportation to and from work. I knew without the responsibly of the regular routine of work, left to my own vices and lifestyle that has so many times keep me from loved ones and family and completely reliant on the department of corrections to medicate my mental illness, I wouldn't last long in the land of the free. I'm absolutely positive my parole officer would absolutely agree with this narrative.

On a visit with Matthew, which I continued to build a relationship with, knowing we would only have the evening, we went to the video store to rent a movie. I had much to learn about raising another human so it was most often trial by error.

I, in a younger age, had read the well-known books by C.S. Lewis, the chronicles of Narnia. Reflecting, on the joy, I had received, I would only consider that little Matt would also enjoy the picture show. I guess honesty is in order here; I really rented the movie for my own curiosity.

After arriving back at home, we prepared to watch the flick. Within the first ten minutes it was clear little Matt was, in no way, enjoying the blockbuster, I had so gallantly rented. I never considered fawns with goat hooves may be a little much for the kid. So what did I do? I became a spoiled kid again and threw a fit, ejected the movie from its playing device and lobbed it at my young little boy. It was to

31

sharpen the image for you, it was like two kids fighting over toys. No matter how embarrassed I am, I would have to give the prize of winning, to little Matt. I will have you know, I was plagued with regret.

In, raising Matthew, I must give his mother all do credit, for most often, I acted as a child myself. She was the one, thank god, that acted with consistency and was, no doubt, the most responsible one.

Matthews's mom had a past with Theresa, obviously due to interactions with me. I should clearer. Matthews's mother was working a job and taking care of Matthew, when I met Theresa. She knew that Theresa and I most often, as an unwritten rule, it was fully knowledgeable, that I would be indulging, in the carnal pleasures, and using heavy drugs. This wasn't a thought his mother would care to think on. It wasn't a far cry to consider I most often got inebriated for unknown lengths of time while in the company of Theresa. Of course this was my own doing, to be not misunderstood. She was correct in her assumptions. Before this last incarceration, I had overdosed on heroin and Staci, Matthews's mother, and Theresa were both in attendance at the hospital, upon my resuscitation after near death. It doesn't take a rocket scientist to see the dilemma; or where there may have been hard feelings. If anything could be said on my behalf, I loved them both; but explain that and get away without being assaulted, am a sure trick!

This, I feel, should give you a broadened idea, of when and why rules had been specified, when, Matthew, my son, was with me for my weekly day off; it was to remain a father son ordeal. On one Saturday evening, I was hanging out with Matthew and the downstairs neighbor's son had made his appearance. Matthew and he decided to build a fort of blankets, using my bedroom. This seemed an average activity for young kids to do. But Matthew comes running out from to back bedroom where he and the boy were carrying on something fierce. As Matthew reached the living room, I asked, "What is all the commotion about?" Now mind you the apartment door is wide open. Matthew bellows, "He bit me!" He then pulls down his pants to his ankles and bares me his bruised, teeth imprinted, bite marked buttocks. At the same moment the neighbor comes up the stairs turns the corner and stands in the doorway in the midst of me inspecting the damage to my kids butt. Can you say awkward? Go ahead and laugh, because if it would have been anyone else but me; I would have taken stock of the situation and would have also, been laughing hysterical. It sure reminds me, life sure has its moments.

Soon the lies began to form when Matthew and Theresa's visits began to correlate. For the adults, intoxication was what was planned for dinner. I began to play the juggling act and I, truly, sucked at it.

As time passed, I no longer felt compelled to keep my appearance in the factory. Now in control of my paychecks, I can only say my personal demons: addiction, bliss, euphoria; whatever you so choose to associate my behavior with, soon became one of dependency.

From association of peers of the same like mind, the frequency of sick days, and the need to leave the factory early, excuses were becoming hard to finagle. Of course by this point Theresa more or less moved in to the apartment. She would most the day sleeping and waiting in anticipation for me to come home from work to tend to the business of running down the dealer in order to medicate, which was now a daily need in order to function in a normal every day sociological living.

Other days Theresa would drop me off at work with high hopes of the relief the drug would grace my day with a bit earlier. Then the inevitable day came when she never made it to pick me up from work, and without a phone call to assure me she was in route I ultimately would need to find another way home.

The physical need for the drug crept in, yet there was no contact from Theresa. The night, all alone, sweating and kicking, due to the absence of the allotted amount of the dope in my system, dragged on and on. In my conscious, I was pleading to hear the phone ring with the update that the woman would be gliding in shortly with the relief the drug promised to give.

Instead, I managed to rally up a lift to the factory, and though, I am sure it was painfully obvious I battled to maintain. By now I was worth only a third of the work load in comparison to when I had the structure of the institution.

When I finally made it back to the house, after a terrible day at work, I found she had made it back to the apartment, minus the vehicle that I so much needed for transportation, and to have access to the drug I was now so dependent upon to function which was now calling the shots as to my responsibility in a sociological member of society. Theresa's story was that the car just died on her and she was unable to manage to restart the engine. She was unable to recall what street or avenue the stranded vehicle was to found. The fact that she was neither in possession of the drug or the monies I had left her with, which was the whole reasoning she had borrowed the vehicle to her in the first place.

Now it doesn't take a rocket scientist to come to terms with reality that the probability, she had intention on the score, had been honest, but what had transpired, was, more than likely, a story more on the lines of her over consumption and through a series of unfortunate events, sad to say; she most likely borrowed the car or rented it. Thus with some truth of the story, the car had been abused, while she was over stimulating her brain.

Unfortunately, becoming part of this lifestyle, these, sometimes, crippling situations, happening at what would seem the worst times, becomes often a regular occurrence. The nature, of the beast, is once one has used or are heavily using, though your mind is heavily sedated, once again, anything you possess; whatever it may be, can and will be taken or lost to you at some point, including memories of a particular event.

I tried my best, although, I was already experiencing the tornado, to hold on to the factory job, but the day came that I showed up late to work after buying yet another car, which in all likelihood, I had been the victim of yet another lemon, that I had purchased, under, or better understood, with my own reality goggles, or so I thought. After thinking, I had dodged a bullet, because I had been playing hooky, trying to kick the bad habit, that without the intoxication the needle brought, to be unable to function without, I was now informed that my services would no longer needed.

It seems as I recall Theresa, by her own choice she began to arrange her own transportation and come into her own means. With no ill intent, the only words to actively convey, is to say that Theresa was very able in the art of seduction. In the lifestyle of a drug addict often the lines of morality can be blurred by only what can be named as desire.

Fortunately, I was able to apply for unemployment. The rigid structure and hours, often unbearable temperatures, seem to have given to my attempt to sociological behaviors.

Unfortunately, the unemployment payment would not be enough for me to pay all my utility bills, car registration and rent. But without possessing much in the amount of monies, I was still managing the abilities to supply myself a fix of heroine. I often sold my belongings or anything else of value including: jewelry or anything accumulated from hard work.

Often due, to having in my possession, a valid driver's license, with auto insurance, and legal registration, I was able to peddle services of transportation, in exchange for the much needed drug.

Drug use can and will take all stability from oneself in the blink of an eye. With Theresa's help I was able to pack my apartment into boxes and garbage bags. Excluding the furniture, I sure thought myself ready to go; possibly due, to the drug induced haze, I was in. I was a walking, talking mess, to caution yourself by.

Wisdom is earned with trials in time. Struggles that have one to falter, builds character. The resilient get back up when thy fall. I jumped in the car and scored some dope.

Chapter 03

"Men are not gentle, friendly creatures, wishing for love, which simply defend themselves if attacked...A powerful desire for aggression has to be reckoned, as part of their endowment."

-Sigmund Freud

Being just recently released from prison, I was very bad, at making good or wise choices. As life had been, at a time before this last incarceration, I had always, had my sweet grandmother's home, to run to, when I fouled things up. Grandma's money always fixed financial loss; but I still hadn't learned how to be responsible, and I was old enough to know better.

My grandmother was now in assisted living; she had sold her home and the faucet that used to flow money had dwindled to a mere drip. The glorious days of basking under a cold fountain with sheer delight were gone. In its place was a debilitating evil of my own construction.

My parents, by adoption, whom I give great credit—that being another tale to tell—lived in the state of New York. Dad had taken to consulting. You see, for the last couple weeks, I had not been answering my telephone. I would, more likely, text. By texting I could hide the groggle in my throat, from the effects, of the heroine, I was using. You cannot have lived with family, without them knowing the trepidations in your life. I had to beg for food, cause, in a short time, I had lost my job, my bank account, and my hope.

It still amazes me that I thought; I could pull it off, using again, before anyone would know. Mom and dad sent a gift card that would allow me to fill my refrigerator and cupboards full, of food; but all my dishes, silverware, and pans had been, already, half packed. It was more like, placed in plastic bags, scattered about, in the dining room.

The walls were pressing in. Theresa was spending more tie with me which seems to be just how she tended to engage me. The closer I got to the edge, the closer she got to me. My depression had me tooth and nail.

I sold the food card for half price, so I could purchase another bag of comforting bliss-heroine.

I, now, had a car that would only fit, what it would fit, no money, no registration, making the car illegal to drive, and nothing but burned bridges for miles. I had, only, been out of prison for three months. Whoever said, "If you close one door another opens", is a liar.

In sheer desperation, I called my brother, Randy, who lived a couple miles away from the apartment. Back to irresponsibility, was the understanding, my brother could see from afar. When I hung up the phone, after giving him my interpretation, of the story, he made some calls regarding, a roof, to put over my head. Himself, after being released from jail, he had utilized a rooming house before graduating to the apartment he lived in with his girlfriend, at the time, named Jenny.

Chapter 04

"Unfortunately, there is no doubt, about the fact, that, man is, as a whole, less good as he imagines himself or wants to be. Everyone carries a shadow, and the less it is embodied, in the individual's conscience life, the blacker, the denser, it is."

-Carl Jung

It doesn't take a psychology major, to ascertain, that use of addictive, mind altering chemicals, can and will exacerbate mental illness. As the law of gravity and basics physics will tell you, "What goes up, must come down." After so many years by living a lifestyle of an addict, and by completing the many rehabilitative programs; I have learned that in the mental sphere of living on drugs, I know, by example, that when you get high, that much more, above a stable consciousness; coming down, one measures, quite a number, of degrees, below the normal degree, leading to a mindset comparable to the psychological term, depression.

Though in certain terms, we ate, had clean clothes to wear, and to all appearances, moderately healthy; but mental stability, certainly, had been thrown to the wind.

My visits with my son, Matthew, were taken and no longer allowed, for Matthews mother knew, by my example that I was no longer stable, what so ever, and, by all probability, I was back to using heavy drugs and back to, again hanging around unsavory individuals and overall irresponsible and reckless.

Theresa would often wander about on her walks and frequently disappear, sometimes, for days at a time. During these periods, I never left the room, unless to use the rooming houses shared facilities, in which by some stroke of luck, I felt confident enough to bathe, notwithstanding. This is, for certain, is a behavior often share by the mentally ill.

I missed or rescheduled mandatory meetings with my parole agent. Most often, in realization, that, if my agent did a drug screen for chemical abuse, I was sure to test dirty-meaning fail miserably. This was a jail able offense; for it was a violation of my rules of parole, or supervision. It was evident that all I was accomplishing, was to dig my own hole. I was, no longer, finding joy in the simplest actions of living life on life's terms. I began to eat less and less. Reading, watching movies and even intimacy were no longer desirable.

Sad but true, suicide began, as an idea, to capture my thoughts. Soon I was caught up in thoughts to plan the ultimate escape. There is no thought of anyone else's feelings, or the impact that this behavior would have on family or ones close to you. The act itself is purely selfish and without reason.

Theresa, months earlier, had been diagnosed as diabetic, and as a result was prescribed injectable insulin.

Isn't it ironic that from my first idea of the use of drugs, being a loaded syringe, I was now planning, the exit, through a tool that brought life for one, would be the tool, to deliver the dose to extinguish life? So on one evening when Theresa decided to go out and about, I took her insulin, out of the refrigerator, where it was stored, filled a syringe, and injected it into my muscle. With certain belief, I would slip away, out from the shadow of depression; I laid in bed, with belief that my breath would finally escape me, once and for all.

I was unaware of how long I slept, but was awakened, by relentless banging, which upon consciousness, I realized, to be someone at the door. When I finally got out of bed, it was my brother, Randy, I found to be the culprit. Upon opening the door, with one look at me, he pushed his way into the room. I guess, God had a different plan, in store, for my life.

Randy had brought me food, and the most legal of my addictions, cigarettes.

The brand of insulin, I later found out, was insulin, that dispersed, through the human body, slowly, giving the body a chance, for it, to metabolize.

Chapter 05

"The greater the power, the greater the abuse."

-Edmund Burke

Pushing fate is a big deal, when once achieved, there is no turning back. Death is a door, once opened, cannot be closed. But, the only hell close to that, in my opinion, would be to tempt the parole officer. When you turn your life upside down, you, most definitely, have changed total appearance, and, most the time, as I've heard, your psychology is no longer structured. The parole officer that deals in criminal psychology, and, not to mention, eighty clients a week, has been trained, to notice these differences, plainly professed.

So now there are no more excuses. The drug tests cannot always be false positives. I had been tested, every time I reported. I did make it to her office with a back pack of excuses. None, of which, she was buying.

On this occasion, she left me sitting in the waiting room, and it must have been going on thirty minutes, which is not the regular routine. But, because, this time, I had showed up, after missing each rescheduled appointment, I took to the understanding, that she was teaching me a lesson on keeping appointments. That was, until, two uniformed police officers entered the building and walked straight over to the chair I was seated in. This is when they ordered me to stand up and began to pat me down, obviously, looking for weapons or what may, of any illegality, that, I might possess, on my person. I was cussing to myself, praying to God, that, I had checked my pockets, before attending this appointment. This was a regular routine, to be sure, that, I didn't possess any loaded syringes, of illegal substance, being too high, to realize.

My pockets were empty.

"Matthew," the officer stated. I said, "Yeah". As he pulled each of my arms behind my back he informed me, "Your parole officer is revoking your parole. So you will be taken to the sheriff's department and booked into the county jail." "Do you have, anyone, that, you need to be notified?" my parole agent inquired, as she stepped out from her office. "Yeah, if you would please, call Theresa, at my phone number, to inform her, I would appreciate it." I returned.

I knew that within a couple of hours, the sweats, shakes, and body pain would be my new reality. That feeling and knowledge is about the most sobering event. As psychology goes, even the criminal that has been in and out of prison, knows, that within the next three days adapting is one hell of a roller coaster, and I was on my way.

Withdrawal consists of: insomnia, sweating, the whole body shaking in fits, upset stomach, diarrhea, body aches, and the running of the nose, most comparable to a leaky spicket. Heroine can be extinguished from the body, within about three days. It depends on the amount of water, you are able to process. Cocaine withdrawal is not a physical ailment. Moodiness is definitely a symptom. Some do experience insomnia, but for the most part, you can just sleep it off. Don't be mistaken if using cocaine on a regular basis, it is now well entrenched as a behavior problem, to be considered.

By the end of the first week, my parole agent had come to see me, with a list of rule violations from absconding, which is defined as missing appointments, use of illicit street drugs, and failure to keep agent informed of my living arrangements, being that, I had failed, to inform her, that Theresa had been staying with me, which she found out once she came in contact with Theresa via telephone. Her recommendation was revocation of my community release, in order for me to rid my body of the toxins or "dry out". This was the suggested results according to the guidelines of Department of Corrections. The final result was that I was jailed for a period of six months.

For informational purposes, I can, only, inform you, as to what lays ahead by interpretation of my mind, in the initial days, experienced from the separation from society. I would lose my unemployment, obviously, for I would be unable to look for work. Also, I would, no doubt, lose my room, at the rooming house, unable to pay rent.

Then during a visit, which in the jail I was housed in was via tele visit-mostly a phone and a monitor, in which I could see my visitor- Theresa came, to see me, one Saturday during visiting hours. She informed that her father had paid the rent and she would still be living there, for the time being. She, then, proceeded to informed me, that she was "late" getting her monthly cycle. She then informed me that she hadn't had her regular monthly cycle in three months. Of course, I had been so preoccupied in my own foolishness; I surely, would have noticed the neglect of having to buy tampons. As with any child, the thought of children, is extremely uplifting. Of course, that is after you get over the initial shock. My realization that a much needed lifestyle change was needed. I wasn't keeping up with my responsibilities of Matthew. Regardless, I was still excited.

Before long, I was transferred from the jail to the state prison to serve out the remainder of my time.

Theresa soon moved in with her parents. I was able to call a couple times a week to keep up to date on how she was getting along. Soon, after a number of refused phone calls, it began, to dawn on me; she was, evidently, spending more time away from her parent's home. Times when I was able to contact her, she only said that she was okay and that she went out sometimes, to shed the irritation, of the feeling, of being cooped up in the house all the time.

The revocation of my community supervision, due to several failed urinalysis, by default, expressing that my drug habits were far from under control; but, maybe, a couple of months to "dry' me out was cause to separation from society.

I met a guy close in age, while in the jail. Time, out of society, is, to be completely honest, just boring. The best you can do is play card games, eat well, and; although the feeling is loneliness, it doesn't hurt, to talk with others that are in the same sinking boat, that you're in. My new acquaintances name was Bobby. Bobby made lite of time, always cracking a joke, of finding humor, often found in the likes, of the same drug addled mind, of the people, we most often associate with. There have only been few people in life that I have come across, in the same situation, contending in time imprisonment, that I cared enough to write down their information and possibly contact after release. Bobby was one of these individuals.

After I finished my short stay in prison, I, really, had no real plans of where I would stay, but, logically, I imagined I would be near, if not living with Theresa. On the day of my release, I was informed, by the sergeant, in control of my release, that there was an individual in the parking lot awaiting my exit.

I went out into the lot, and my eyes drew into focus Theresa's fathers van. A casual wave of his arm, out the vehicle window, motioning me near, was a welcomed site. As I approached the van, I came to notice, Theresa wasn't in the front seat. I went around to the passenger's side door, and opened the door, enough to fling my body, onto the seat. I closed the door from the cool winter weather.Her father made small talk as we headed east to familiar counties. As we pulled into town, he informed me that Theresa was in labor. Automatically, I figured we were on our way to the hospital. Instead we pulled into the lot of the Salvation Army, and he put it to me like this, "Theresa doesn't want you to come to the hospital. She has a friend there now. You can call, periodically, to see how things go." This wasn't the plan, remotely close, to the idea, of how I imagined things to be. I guess, plans change and change they do.

Chapter 6

"All the world is a stage. All the men and women merely players. They have their exits and their entrances.And one man, in his time, plays many parts."

-William Shakespeare

Living at the Salvation Army was quite the eye opener. It was, often, quite aggravating to have to co-exist the evening hours, because, I imagine, being awakened early, and expected to be off the premises by eight o'clock in the morning, the hygiene, of people, left much to be desired of. I had never been homeless before. In prison, a shower of warm water is something to do, besides the obvious self-cleaning, and, of course to cool off from the summer heat. It is often nature's own way to wash stress and the aches and pains away.

In the Salvation Army, there are all walks of life but some you could not even drag into the shower. The smell was absolutely terrible. Often, the dire need of a shower was so needed to wash the funk out of your nose and off your body that seem to have saturated you just from being near some individuals.

Being freshly released from prison and trying vigorously, to steer clear of the whole drug scene, as well as the lifestyle, in order to stay out of the frigid coolness of season, after leaving the roof of the Salvation Army; I would walk a couple blocks to the Sobriety Club for warmth and company.

A hot cup of coffee to warm the gullet, and there was always someone to sit with and converse for company.

Theresa bore a son she named Aiden. She did end up staying at her parents' house after the delivery at the hospital. Our conversations over the telephone would only be in regards to that little boy. He was born jaundice. Of course, I was concerned for he was my little boy.

Theresa had my clothes from living at the rooming house at her parents' home. I used that as an excuse to get close to my new born child. It seemed there was no other way, for she seemed, to me, at the time, to be, what seemed to me try to avoid our coming together. My plan worked and the following day, I had a friend of mine drive me to the country, to meet my son for the first time. I held my small child in my arms; I was overcome with emotion. It must have been an hour I held him, before he had to be placed back in his crib to be placed under an ultra-violate light, to ward off the jaundice.

Theresa and I talked about the relationship she had chosen to undertake in my absence. She told me she really had feelings for the guy and, in truth, what else was there to say about that. I left that day sad, for the separation, but with full intention of being a part of the life of that little boy, that innocent infant, named Aiden.

Though out of prison, I was still under supervision by a parole agent, at least, for the remainder six months of my sentence, given from the judge. It was required of me to participate in an outpatient drug treatment program. At this time in my life, I had attended, at best guess, in the realm of seven or eight, drug prevention programs. They would last a period of eight to twelve weeks on the average. Prepare to be quite bored from the familiarity of programming, I, obediently, attended, as required, by the order of my parole agent.

I was sitting at the table, with a completely negative attitude, pondering what kind of trouble I could find; although none would be accepted if I returned to the Salvation Army, under the influence, of anything for that matter, when my attention was consumed with the individual that just walked through the door. It was my friend, I had met in the jail months earlier. It was Bobby.

With having a friend there made the whole process of keeping attention more pleasurable, because my attitude was now better. Iy wasn't long before Bobby's obnoxiousness won me over by spurring humor. Bobby was the kind of guy that lit the room with his candor.

After class, Bobby and I hung out, catching up, as we chain smoked cigarettes. Before long, Bobby had to ask the million dollar question, "Can you still score?" "Of course, I can," I said. This, of course, was regarding my available connections for the sparkly controlled substance cocaine.

It wasn't that night, but soon, due to my connections with multiple dealers of the drug; I soon began to deal bobby large amounts of cocaine.

I still hung out at the Sobriety Club. I had no choice but to remain sober to reside at the Salvation Army. I soon met a Goth chick at the club. She had straight, black hair with cropped bangs, and an attractive slim figure. She worked at the club part time. She worked behind the bar serving coffee and conversation. I made that club my second home. I kind of stalked her, but more or less struck by some youthful crush.

My brother, Randy, also, was in contact with a couple of dealers, and living in the same city, I utilized his resourcefulness. I spent a lot of time at his house when I wasn't at the club or the homeless shelter. Then one day, upon Randy opening the door, to allow me entrance, I noticed what appeared to be a dent on his forehead. To me, it looked like someone had grazed his skull with a hammer. He was in the battle of the mind, and looked like death warmed over.

I didn't say much, but followed him up the staircase to his apartment upstairs, on the second floor. After coming through the upstairs door, I locked it behind me securing the apartment as anyone in the drug business knows securing the door may give you the needed extra moments to flush the drugs down the toilet in the event the police come and kick in the door; or, in the event, someone kicks in the door, in the attempt to rob you, you have a second or two to hide the drugs and money and acquire a weapon to defend yourself. After securing the door, I asked him blatantly, "What the fuck happened to your head?" He went on to explain he had went on to the city with his friend Paul to acquire a reasonably large amount of cocaine.

Upon arrival he went into the house, he inquired, reasonably, to the whereabouts of his dealer. Believing that the individual was in the dealers spot reliable and trustworthy, he began by asking if the amount of cocaine he had made plans to pick up was available for the transaction, since he had made this trip to the city. The dealer pulled out a large zip lock of pre-bagged small packages of random sizes of the drug.(If you break down a sizeable amount into separate bags differing by weight, you can charge a higher amount on each bag, so anyone purchasing the product would rather buy bulk than prepackaged product) Upon seeing this, Randy seen that the man knew that under the conditions the demand would most often win out, and the product purchased at a higher rate.

Randy said he decided to wait until a later date and time to acquire the lower price and divide the coke into packaging himself, and in turn cover more of his own usage. He went on with the details of the next events.

Departing, the frustration was evident on this unknown dealer's countenance.

Being in the city, Randy was aware of the danger of street thugs or even law enforcement, especially coming out of a known drug house. It doesn't take a rocket scientist to know; simply guilty by association could be cause enough for speculation to law enforcement, to presume that drugs were involved.

Walking to the running vehicle, Randy failed to see the hooded figure come from behind, yelling profanities, brandishing a firearm, demanding any and all monies in Randy's pockets. Standing sideways, evidently, not moving fast enough, for the hooded mugger fires the pistol. At less than ten feet apart, at point blank range, the mugger unloaded five shots.

At this point, Paul keeping the vehicle warm, and ready for transport, fled upon viewing the situation, with firm belief that the bullets had found their mark.

The mugger standing with unbelief, with a now empty gun, proceeded to use the butt of the gun, to pistol whip Randy, causing the dent in his forehead, and bleeding down his face and soaking onto his clothes.

Randy went on to tell me, the mugger then ran away.

He said he was pretty dazed, but he, automatically, began walking the main road looking for a phone to use, to call his ride Paul, so he would come pick him up and he could live another day. After being passed by multiple times by patrolling police vehicles, Randy, a with blood covered face and saturated bloody clothes, was ignored. Even with flailing arms and pleads for help, ignored. He went on to say, he didn't even know if he had been shot or how badly he was hurt.

After finding a pay phone, he expressed he was able to call Paul, who was halfway home, convince him to turn around, and pick him up at the gas station. It took a half hour before he could feel the warm of the heater in the safety of the car. After checking his body over, Randy could not believe the fact that no bullet had pierced his body.

I said, "So Paul left you, huh?"

He replied, "He thought I was dead".

His next words were, "I am going on a vacation away from this shit." My brother's girlfriend, Jenny, came from the bed room carrying a bag which I imagined was the clothes she packed for the trip. Within a moment or two there was a car horn outside Randy's apartment. It was his friend Paul. They were going to see Paul's mother, who was living in some town off the Mississippi River, a couple hours away.

A week later Randy came home to pack up his apartment. He called me on the telephone to inform me he was moving. When I asked why, he said," I was lucky not to die. I think it was divine intervention." He went on to explain that he had fallen in love with the nature of the country, and he carried on about how the eagles fed off fish on the river edge as it thawed. He was exuberant as he recalled the sight. He went on to say, "Matt, this is my second chance, you are more that welcome to utilize this apartment, for the rent is paid until the first of the month. He left a chair, a television, video player, and movies to watch.

Chapter 07

"Each relationship strengthens a character in you."

-M. Merdok

I stayed at the Salvation Army, rather than stay at my brother, Randy's empty apartment. I would not have been able to pay the rent, because at that time I had no income. My parole officer wanted me to stay clean and I had no faith in my choices, so I volunteered to enter into a volunteer drug rehabilitation program.

The Salvation Army allowed you one night of not returning, or to be in attendance rather, before they gave your bed away. I took advantage of this. I took the Goth girl, Julie, out and we had fun in company, for it was a double date. Our part of the date went into the evening, never ending til morning. Yes, we spent the night in the embrace of each other's arms. It was so enjoyable that I spent the next evening never leaving the apartment. We had created a bond.

The next day was my agreed upon date for me to start the inpatient drug rehabilitation drug program. Before I made it to the doors of the program, I, by chance, bumped into a friend that presented me an offer to help him do some demolition for a remodeling company. So now I was employed part time.

I saw Julie almost every night when I would visit the Sobriety Club, which was thought quite highly of seeing I was in a drug program.

For the next couple of months, during the daylight hours, I submerged myself in compliance with the program. Some

afternoons I spent in my room at the rehab painting, for though I am no professional I do enjoy art. Evenings that I didn't work with my friend, I spent a couple of hours at Julie's house in her company, or followed her to work at the club. Through long talks we built a decent relationship.

I stuck with the rehab program, for it lasted to the day of my release from the community custody of my supervising parole agent of the Department of Corrections. I graduated by completing my parole as was the intent of utilizing the drug program. That was the day I moved in to live with Julie in her apartment.

I had acquired a phone for convenience, and it was within days of my release, I received a call from my buddy Bobby. Bobby took me to the bar to commemorate the event of no longer having a supervisory authority to any longer answer to. The beers were cold, and Bobby was a frequent patron, so there were many free drinks and pleasant conversation with others he knew. Of course, at one point, when Bobby came back from the bar restrooms, he asked, "Can you make that call for me now?" I had been expecting it and knew that question was coming. A phone call later we were on our way to the city to score some high grade, next to pure cocaine.

We stopped at a friend of Bobby's after the business had been tended to. Bobby's friend had the name of Kevin. I soon learned that Kevin also enjoyed every thing that came along with the lifestyle of cocaine distribution and Kevin was all too happy to meet me. The cocaine I was running was a step below pure and Kevin showed me his operation which consisted of cutting the product with acetone and vitamin B complex. We made three bricks into five increasing profits three hundred percent. That wasn't even counting the piles of money I was making on the original deal.

I kept a job with Pete in demolition, and when I ran into my old friend Kenny walking the streets one day after not seeing him for a couple years; I got him a job with Pete in demolition too.

With Bobby and Kevin's constant demand, often up to a couple of runs a week, I acquired a vehicle for work, but, also, I, once again,

Before long Bobby who wasn't into heroine prior now found himself a new habit, the staggering effects of heroine. Now, although, I still got the call for the coke; I was now getting numerous calls for heroine. Heroine knows no prejudice. It will addict all walks of life: male or female, rich or poor, black, white, yellow or blue. Kevin, Bobby, Julie, Kenny, and I included, all became quite addicted.

I often tried to contact Theresa, to plan a day to see Aiden. Theresa was often unavailable to me. Then the day came that I was served court custody papers, from the sheriff's department, for a scheduled appearance in front of a court judicial.

I took Julie with me, to the specified court date. Julie didn't trust men in general, this being due to a past of abuse. So taking Julie to my court date, I thought this would make her less leery, considering the situation. It didn't matter, with still all precaution taken, we were both quite uncomfortable.

I was excited, upon arrival, for I had looked forward to the court date, because I could at least see my son Aidan. I had expected Theresa to have brought him, but, to my dismay, she did not. Instead she brought her older sister Vicky. I later found out that Theresa had left Aidan unattended, while she left the house, at some point. The most probable factor was that she had intended to leave, for just a little while, to relieve a drug addled craving and as drugs tend to do, she lost track of time. Do to this irresponsible event, an agreement had been taken, upon, where with, Theresa, avoiding penalties of the law, awarded her sister Vicky temporary custody, in hopes that Theresa would grasp the gravity of the situation.

The judge ordered a DNA blood test, for paternity, to ensure Aidan was my son. Another court date was set to resume custody hearings, in which time Vicky would not allow me any access to my son, Aidan.

My relationship with Julie flourished. She was ten years my senior; in some humorous sense, a cougar. I still recall the morning, she asked me how old I was. I was cooking eggs scrambled, I remember, for she had asked me not to season the eggs, and the way I saw it was if someone was going to cook breakfast for you, you just be thankful. Anyhow after she asked how old was and I answered with thirty one; she kind of got mad. She went on to explain, she had a son that was not much younger that myself. Personally, I think she weighed the scales in her mind and our intimacy in the sack, me being a stallion, won the prize.

Not long after a revealing episode, Julie opened a door of realization to me. She explained to me that she had a mental illness diagnoses as bipolar, hyper sexuality (which was just as well), and she also was diagnosed with Post traumatic stress disorder, cause by physical abuse by a past boyfriend. I had a past of mental illness but never gave it much substance for I did not understand it. I naïvely believed, if you chose, you could mentally override the disorder. It had never dawned on me that I had been self-medicating to relieve my own symptoms. When given pills, I just thought they had been a crouch to help me cope, how ignorant I had been. My diagnosis had been incomplete for there really was ever a long enough period off of drugs to accurately diagnose me. I took stock in my cougar's revelation.

Julie had quit her job at the Sobriety Club, not for any other reason than, as she said, it wasn't right to work there and be using illicit street drugs. Julie also had severe migraines, painful enough to cause her nausea and vomiting, and after several visits to the emergency room she was prescribed morphine tablets. Of course this was just added onto our daily tally of narcotics.

Chapter 08

"He who has a why to live, can bear with almost any how."

-Friedrich Nietzsche

Then the day of court for the custody of Aiden came to pass. For the life of me, I don't remember if Theresa was present at the courthouse that day. It had been heavy on my mind, for I was at war with myself, regarding the correct action to take, for Aiden's well-being was at stake. My thoughts were on the line as: what kind of person, having drug dependence, having two other children that I was neglecting being an adequate responsible party and what should I do in the best interest for an innocent child.

I distinctly recall Aiden's aunt pulling me aside and, with tears in her eyes, asked me, to please, make the responsible decision, to allow her and her husband, to adopt Aiden, raise him with religion, and care for him financially; which I was in no way capable, to do, at the present time. I was angry and infuriated.

On that day, I put my past, my youth, and knowing what it was like to be abandoned, I too, as was done to me, I abandoned my child. As I signed away my parental rights of Aden, Vicky placed a stipulation on me that i was to have no contact with Aiden before his eighteenth birthday.

It was not long after that, I was visiting a friend of mine named Paul, and he informed me that Theresa had died of an overdose, in the apartment of the complex he was currently living in.

A person does a drug because it makes them feel good. I did heroine to feel comfortable in my own skin, to forget my sin. When doing heavy street drugs on a regular basis, it has been pointed out to me, there is a change in a person like night and day. You live life lawless; soon you become, often with no emotion, psychotic without feeling or emotion.

The only real tangible thing I had going for me, was Julie or so I thought. As I look back, I can remember what drew her towards me, other than just getting out of jail and she was female; it was that that straight, black, hair that boxed her face, due to the short bangs. She walked a miniature dog, rat terrier. She was sleek and enticing. I am in no way saying that my sons were not important at the time, but Matthew's mother, being a protective woman of her child, wouldn't allow me to see him until I showed some stability. I don't blame her. My demolition job had to become my rock.

It was on an odd occurrence that I noticed a boil that grew in size in my underarm. I went to the hospital to get some advice for it was painful. The doctor decided that the boil should be lanced. In the process of lancing the boil, the doctor had used a numbing agent named Lidocaine. However, the fist injection didn't do the trick in numbing the area sufficiently, so the doctor took more medicine out the bottle to insure reduced pain. Before leaving the hospital, that day, I stole that bottle of Lidocaine.

Randy, my older brother, would soon call explaining, he would soon be visiting. This is better understood as, he wanted me to set up the cocaine deal, seeing he was not in the loop any longer and did not know which dealer he could trust. After meeting up with my brother and several dealings in cocaine later, two days had spent and now due to having gotten any sleep, I was having severe pain in my jaw and ear drum.

Remembering that I still had the bottle of Lidocaine, I used a syringe and sucked up some medicine out the pharmaceutical bottle. I injected the medicine into my cheek believing it would eventually numb the area that was ailing me. I continued this injection several times for the next two days in which I still hadn't given my body the time to rest and recuperate the beating I had been giving it. My brother finally fell asleep on the couch in mine and Julie's home.

My face had started to give me excruciating pain, so I went to the bathroom to take a look. What no one had told me was that my face had swollen on the right side to the size of a foot ball, not a soft ball but a foot ball. I hurried to the bedroom to tell Julie that it was necessary to go to the hospital. "Wait until the morning and we will go to the hospital," Julie stated.

I tightened the muscles in my face and in the corner of my mouth my lip split and a thick, cottage cheese, type density of mucus oozed out of my lip. I think Julie about puked and though the smell of body odor from the past days expenditures, with out a shower, was vile, it was nothing compared to the smell of that mucus coming out of my face.

We made it to the hospital after a little struggle with Julie. Upon entering the hospital and registering at the front desk, one look at me, and I was hurried into a room and a doctor was immediately paged. A doctor was soon to my right side of the bed wishing to press on the infected area. He waited til I was extremely high from the injection given to me through an IV a nurse has worked into my arm. The doctor informed me that when I was last at the hospital, I hadn't stayed   at the hospital long enough, but the test results from the culture of my lanced boil was conclusive to a staph infection commonly known as MRSA. He went on to explain that this is most likely the cause of the infection in my face.

The doctor told me this is a severe case and as soon as I agreed to stay and be treated he ordered more pain medication. Whether it was due to the interaction with all the street drugs that had intoxicated me for the last week, or that my psych was close to collapse, as soon as the drugs ordered from the doctor were injected I became combative with the hospital staff. Julie later informed me that I had created quite the scene before the staff fought back injecting a tranquilizer into the IV to disable me in a matter of seconds.

I was put on a heavy dose of antibiotics after a succession of different antibiotics proved ineffective. In medical terms, I believe, they explained it as resistant. I slept for a number of days and was told that I had been real lucky; and if I hadn't come in when I did, the infection would have gone septic and very likely killed me. I asked what the doctors meant and he had a far away look in his eye. then he turned to me and said, "Your blood system Matt, your blood system would have been compromised, resulting in death."

I soon noticed that Julie had pulled another chair next to the bed, and had stayed with me. She was dressed in a yellow gown with a blue mask covering her face. It then dawned on me everyone that came into to give me medication, or food, or even anyone that came in to check the machine, that monitored my vitals that persisted in beeping every time I moved, was also suited up wore the coverings.

Randy, my brother, came up to the hospital. I am sure that Julie had informed him that I would be in the hospital. He himself had spent recovering at the apartment. He informed me that he had to return to the country so he could be released from the addictive pleasures of the city. Through the opiate haze I was experiencing, we hugged and IO watched him leave.

I stayed in the hospital a number of weeks. Julie would leave and come back showered and ready to try and liven me up with her company. Being adequately medicated from the IV morphine drip, I would gobble them up greedily. Junkie love.

Chapter 09

"Then he can worship and be enlarged by his worship, for he can never go beyond this sentiment."

--Ralph Waldo Emerson

After about a month in the hospital, I was released. For the obvious reason Bobby was especially happy, for he again had opportunity through my drug connections. Unlike the locomotive , slowly bring up to speed, I think Bobby's idea was along the lines, he would get enough, so he was never going to run out of the drugs if he had anything to say about it. My disappearance due to the infection seemed to have put a kink in his style.

The seemingly short rides to the city soon turned into whole afternoons, for the quantities were larger and it became a part of the process to cut the drug to avoid overdoses when peddled.

The hospital had released me with a bottle of Vic Odin, and not wishing to regain the opioid habit, Julie and I stayed clear of the possession of heroine

. Thinking this was enough, but not admitting that some was never enough, before long the pills were gone and the need took over. Instead of using heroine the whole idea of using pills was the fact that using pills you always know what you are getting. Unlike heroine, the potency is always known.

One afternoon, on a Friday, my long standing friend, Kenny called to invite me over, to his apartment, which happened to be right around the corner from where Julie and I stayed. The purpose for my mandatory visit, he stated, was that he harbored another old acquaintance, visiting, at his apartment, that he thought I may like to see for old time sake.

Curiosity got the best of me, so I went to stop by. I could smell the distinct odor as soon as I opened the door of the apartment building. The odor was even stronger when Kenny opened the door to my knock.

"Jesus, man opens the window," I exclaimed. The cloud of cocaine smoke rushed out the window in wisps as Kenny wrestled the window open that had been painted shut.

The acquaintance was my old friend that I, in fact, had met through Kenny many years before. His name was Bolts(I know funny name hey?).As our friendship had grown, I had found him to be a trustworthy, and a standup guy. I knew he was homosexual, but as long as he kept his hands to himself, respected that I was not into homosexual activity, we would get along fine. As a matter of fact, earlier in my youth, I would hang out with other friends at his apartment. It was often, that I was under the influence of, the drug, LSD. In taking the drug, I was vulnerable do to the intoxication from the drug, but Boltz had always respected my boundaries. With Kenny, I had always suspected that he had some private relationship with Boltz, but it was neither here nor there to me. I had met them both at a young age and our relationships had lasted over the years. Boltz would often remind me that since meeting me, I had a habit of filling his freezer with large zip locks of marijuana.

It was evident that Kenny, Mark, and Kenny's live in girlfriend, Barb, were extremely high on cocaine. After pleasantries were exchanged, we drank many beers together, and found myself quite tweaked. After what in all intent and purposes, had meant to be a short visit, lasting into the afternoon several hours later, I made my way home no worse for wear.

A day later, on a Sunday afternoon, the doorbell buzzer of the apartment sounded, repeatedly. My nap-time disturbed; it was officially over. I went to the intercom and pressed the button to the down stairs door allowing access to the complex. After a moment later, there was the all too familiar rap on the door, which made me aware that Kenny was the individual responsible for interrupting my nap. Boltz was with Kenny, and it came to me, by their disheveled appearance, that neither of them had gotten any sleep since I had seen them last. They looked strung out.

I invited them into the apartment; although they kinda dragged themselves through the doorway. I made my way to the kitchen and in the freezer was a bottle of Tequila which I produced, for they both looked like they needed to come down. This lasted well into the night.

As the night wore on, Kenny filled me in, on the idea, that he had decided he was going to move in with Mark, and that he and Barb, his girlfriend, had broken up. He went on to inform me, he had just broken up with Barb after an argument because he had spent his entire paycheck on cocaine that weekend. He explained, now didn't have the rent for the room they shared at the rooming house. I, naturally, asked him where she was going to stay, and he informed me that she was going to move back in with her mother.

After the bottle of Tequila was gone, we progressed into drinking the case of beer chilled in the refrigerator.

Now drunk and in a stupor, Kenny depression getting the best of him, broke down and told me, at an earlier date, he had gotten himself in trouble with the police. He went on to inform me that had turned, and was now an informant for the drug task force. He explained, he had already made a number of controlled buys, of narcotics, supervised by the police. Of course my first question was, "Kenny, do I have anything to worry about?" Kenny let out a deep breath and said,"Matt, you're my friend since we were in high school, I would never get you in trouble to save myself." Obviously, this was a relief; however, there was only so much consolation I could give my old friend. I could not save him from himself.

We worked our way through most the beer. Julie and I made our way to the bedroom. From a tender kiss, the fire of desire was spurred. A bit sloppy drunk ourselves, it took a moment longer for us, to shed our clothing. Bodies intertwined, we, in time, found the pleasure we both desired above everything. After, we fell asleep, yet intertwined.

It was four in the morning, I was awakened to the sound of heavy snoring, and not being accustomed to Kenny's sleep habits, I assumed Kenny was getting his much needed rest. I adjusted my sleep position, blocked out Kenny's snoring, cuddled with Julie and soon faded off into my own much needed rest.

Upon awakening, around 9 A.M.,I enjoyed a number of cups of coffee with Julie, which was our routine. The fact I still had a bit of a hang over, I had strong faith in strong coffee. I remember the morning so clearly, due to the fact, whenever we had gone for our regular living needs, such as: toilet paper, light bulbs, cleaning supplies, and the one we seemed somehow to always forget, coffee filters. We had forgotten so often, hidden in the drawer below the coffee maker, we stored a silk scarf of Julies that we had used, on occasion, experimentally, as a theory, in its success as acting as a coffee filter. Of course, with strong desire, there is no shame. In so as much, if nothing else, coffee was served. When I look back, I wonder what others, whom may have visited, often thought of the coffee sodden scarf.

After coffee, again, as our routine, barricaded ourselves in the bathroom, and again, we did what adult coupes do. We exercised passion, and after with a cool refreshing shower, we energized for our day.

The particulars of that morning will never be forgotten. Boltz, who slept on the day bed, in the living room, stirred occasionally. Our next event transpired. It was much to do with the trimming of my hair which the needed trimming was long overdue. Julie broke down and trimmed me when she got sick of looking at "the mountain man". Shortly after cleaning up the hair on the kitchen floor, I through some eggs over easy and some toast together in doing my part to putting some vitamins and sustenance back into my longtime friends.

As the smell of breakfast permeated the apartment, Boltz was the first to pull him together, and was the first to attempt to stir Kenny from the land of the weary. Boltz's next statement will forever be burned into my mind. "Something's wrong," he mumbled.

I walked around the breakfast bar to give Kenny a shove with my foot. "It's noon, ya bum, get up and eat, will ya?" I exclaimed in trying to rouse Kenny from his mode of sleep.

Kenny's body moved to my prod, with a stiff and ridged movement. I muttered, "What the fuck?" And at the same moment of awareness, Boltz announced, "All my Valium is gone!" He held up and shook an empty prescription bottle. The next moments drew on for what seemed an eternity. I pulled the blanket off of Kenny. He was in a fetal position and held a bluish gray sheen to the color of his face. I vaguely recall dialing the emergency number 911, but, it was evident that there was no emanate threat of time, as a barrier, to overcome. The realization settled in. My old friend, Kenny, now lay lifeless, on my living room floor.

As soon as the police and fire department came, they secured the scene. Not long after the coroner arrived to investigate the scene, Julie and I were interviewed. With nothing much to say we were kicked out of the apartment to secure the scene for processing the evidence for a physical investigation. Boltz was interviewed separately, as Julie and I wandered through the town and the apartment was tossed by the authorities with a fine tooth comb.

Julie and I occasioned our home periodically, for the temperature was surely below freezing. It seemed Boltz was being interviewed by several detectives in the hallway up the top stairs. As soon as there was the removal of my old friend's body, which it took the effort of several of the investigators to carry him down the stairs and to the coroner's vehicle, all other personal removed themselves.

Sad as it may sound, when my phone rang, and I saw who was calling; my heart beat excelled at the thought of the much needed bliss that came expectantly with a hook up with Bobby.

Boltz stayed the night.

I imagine after the police had given Kenny's mother the news of her son's death; I was the first she called. I had been known, in his family, from the many years and such a long friendship with Kenny. I surely cannot blame her, for I can only imagine her sorrow and her grief exposed as she screamed at me through the telephone. Many times, for years, she had given Kenny and I, the shake of the head, or the evil eye, when the common occurrence, and with her notice of our dilated eyes and frantic movements, she witnessed in the two of us over the years, as we reveled in our folly.

The cocaine acquired, with Bobby's help, really was not effective; though the use gave Julie, Boltz and myself something else to do rather than sit in shock unable to engage each other.

The funeral was a number of days later, and, of course, I attended. I was sure to pass on silver dollars placed in Kenny's hands, to pay the boatman that would take him to the shores of eternity. It was an end to that dimension of my existence.

That was the last time I seen or heard from Boltz. A couple of weeks later, on the six o'clock news, I viewed a segment which informed me that Boltz was shot dead after an altercation on the city transit system. He evidently attempted to pick up a date, and the fellow took offence. I did not attend his funeral.

Chapter 10

"It doesn't take a lot of strength to let go. It takes a lot of strength to hang on."

-J.C.Watts

"Art is in every human soul." Julie would say. Painting, in the abstract art, has always, as long as I can remember, been a favorite study of mine. All through life, forms of art intrigued me. Whether it was complete color adjustment or base color to contrast, I found joy in the task painting and dreaming of the times in which they had been formed. Since I can remember, the gods and iconic people of old mystified me. The more mystified I became, the harder I sought truth. The simplicity in art, the whole process, of one color, one outline, one brush stroke, could change the whole image. Art, I also found a religion of sorts. It is the simplest form of Nature, and Nature is truth.

Seasons came and went. I continued my sporadic work with my friend Pete in demolition. Use of the word sporadic is due to the fact that I was far from stable. One can only imagine, unless it is the know, that heavy use of drugs with minimal sleep, certainly didn't help the situation. But the core problem, itself, was depression. A shadow that would drown me. The higher the drugs took me, the lower I would come down. In order to ward off the suicidal ideation, it was a physical as well as psychological need to self-medicate.

My brother Randy always gave me the unexpected call, and then showed up a couple of hours later. Of course, it was a drug run for him. He would later explain that after a couple of drink at the bar, in the small town he lived in, he would get the itch to use. Next thing was the three hour drive to come see me. I had become my brother's drug dealer.

Originally, after moving to the country with his girlfriend, you could say the tides changed, and his girlfriend found no peace living in the country, and decided to move back to the city. Randy can be considered a bit codependent, for without a partner he seemed to struggle with depression. As luck would have it, he soon was introduced to a middle aged woman by the name of Regina. She was the sister of his friend Greg. Regina had mental health issues that were on the severe. She suffered from Bi-polar disorder and schizophrenia. The traits of these illnesses were quite evident although being treated by a professional. Randy took it upon himself to do his best in being the best friend he could be towards Regina. A bond was established.

Greg and Regina's father became sick, and after a losing fight with mesothelioma, succumbing to the illness, died. Due to a class action law suit against several manufacturing companies, Regina and Greg were awarded $150,000 apiece.

Randy, since his youth in working for landscape construction, as well as land maintenance, had always wished that one day he could own, his own landscaping company. Regina, after herself, getting to know my brother and his desires, offered him his dream. One day, Regina told Randy to quit his factory job, and handed him $70,000 cash to buy equipment in building his landscape company.

With Randy's past and what seemed like an endless amount of money, it was merely a waiting game until Randy made the trip to visit with a fist full of a surprise. It started with an order, of course, of a quite large amount of cocaine, as well as, an assortment of other heavy narcotics, being prescription pills. Randy rented a motel for himself and got lost for nearly a week. Unfortunately, part of the intended trip had an agenda to see his daughter, my niece, graduate from a prominent private high school. Due to the major side effects, of having a drug induced good time, notwithstanding a lack of sleep, is paranoia, and an insatiable desire to consume more of the powdery substance, cocaine; we missed my niece's, my brother's daughter, Meghan's High school graduation.

Regina, my brother's bank and girlfriend, hadn't participated in this rendezvous but sat patiently at home three and a half hours away. Although, Regina called, repeatedly, but Randy, being intoxicated wouldn't answer the phone but would routinely text her to assure her he was well, I suppose. After that week, Randy took the trip home, no worse for wear but sure a little less rich.

The next week, he called and I could, of course, see through his shenanigans, that no matter what he said, that he was coming with Regina this time to visit and see me. He also informed me with fair warning that, Julie and I were to prepare for a decent weekend, to be spent away from the apartment.

This time it was no small pickup truck but a brand new, right off of the lot, sticker still on the window, Ford Expedition. Looking over the vehicle, I became quite aware this truck had all the new bells and whistles. There had been no expense spared. We followed the routine as the last visit from Randy. We stockpiled the cocaine, and Randy spared no expense when providing the funds for an adequate supply of narcotics, to supply Julie and I the amount needed for our bodily demand of opiates for the weekend and then some. Regina didn't partake in the cocaine use, but fed her own addiction she had to opiates in which I had supplied her. The cash machine never quit ringing and the beat went on.

Next, we met Randy's daughter Meghan and her boyfriend at an exclusive Hotel, which could be considered, top notch, complete with a swimming area with many water slides. It was a neat time spent with family, although very intoxicated. Before Randy was to return home, after leave of Meghan, we visited my dear grandmother who was in an independent living nursing facility. Of course, Grandma was just thrilled to see us. We spent the whole afternoon into the evening visiting, but all too soon it was time to go. Visiting hours were over. Leaving her was emotional. This ancient lady had raised Randy and I through our lives since teenage years. It hurt to put her in the rear view mirror.

The surprises didn't stop there. Instead of dropping Julie and I at home, without warning or even asking if we had other plans, Randy jumped the freeway. He and Regina kidnapped Julie and I, with a promise of a greater surprise and an excuse that we haven't been able to spend enough time with each other. The drive of three and a half hours seemed to never end though we were in continual use of narcotics which had myself quite comfortable. I soon took notice of the bluffs and acres of foliage cascading the bluffs. I was soon lost in the beauty of my brother's world.

We first stayed in Regina's trailer in her spare bedroom. Though sleep eluded us due to the continual use of cocaine; after another day or so Randy, Julie and I seemed to level out and soon sleep followed. Julie and I woke to our stockpile of pills. There would be no detox withdrawals for this adventure. Randy and Regina dined us on grill cooked steaks and boiled lobster. Our visit we were quite spoiled.

Not wishing to leave this heavenly welcome, it was soon time to get back home and pay the rent, for the time had sure passed quickly. We ate breakfast and Randy threw me the keys to his old truck. "Be sure to check the oil every month" is all he said. I gave my brother a hug of gratitude and a tighter hug for old time's sake. He shook my hand and left three hundred dollar bills in my palm. We hadn't managed two miles an d I thankfully passed the village police. I had to wave him over for I was already lost.

Through the next couple of month, I visited often, making the trip myself or at times, picking up my son Matthew. Randy so loved to spoil Matthew. With having no son of his own, I figured why not allow Randy to spoil mine?

Now that we had a vehicle, of course, there were no more issues of transportation. Hopefully there would be no more of unfortunate events such as Julie and I had encountered at an earlier date. We had taken a bus with minimal monies, predestined to be spent on a trip to the moon by use of cocaine. There was a snow warning on the news, we had observed before leaving, but headed not.The bus did a great job of plowing through the large accumulations.

Pulling to our stop, we would have to walk a couple of blocks through the snow to arrive at the dealer's home. We partook of the forbidden fruit, and after use, we made our way back to the bus stop whose route would take us back to the warmth of home. Upon arriving at our designated stop, it took at least an hour and what seemed a lot longer for the bus to finally make it to the scheduled place of pick up. The operator opened the door of the bus and proceeded to inform us that due to the storm all routes were now cancelled. We returned to the dealer's residents and stay the evening. It took till morning for the streets to be plowed enough to allow transportation to proceed as usual. We were very happy to make it home after spending the evening at the kitchen table while the dealer drank whiskey out the bottle, and, as the hours passed, became more and more belligerent while we waited out the storm; because we had not our own transportation. Now this would no longer ever be the issue.

Transportation means a degree of freedom, that, the more fortunate, I feel, most often take for granted. The biggest benefit was having the vehicle so I could have better access to visits with my kid Matt. It was much more versatile for the obvious reasons and less stressful when dealing with Matthew's mother when transportation wasn't an issue.

Matthew's mother, Staci, was most often reasonable regarding visitation with Matthew. Though, it was most often physically evident or rather apparent by loss of weight or raccoon eyes was I had been using heavy street drugs. Staci knew me well. I think she was just happy that Matthew was still able to see me and I made the effort. I think the defining factor was when Matthew came Julie always held her vitality on her sleeve which made Staci more at ease. And often when I would kidnap the kid, with permission to be clear, and take him up to the country to visit and hang out with Randy, Staci also seemed more at ease. I think, because Randy made the effort to change his life for the better, in which to all outside appearances, he had no attachments to the old lifestyle. Maybe, it appeared that he was no longer living in a lawless lifestyle, or it was simply, he had money and new toys that, if he were using heavily, he couldn't afford.

The trips, to visit Randy, in the company of Nature, were, via the highway, often through farmland, the trip was always a thing of beauty. You were guaranteed to see hawks, eagles, cows and the mighty Mississippi river.

Some routes were curvy rounding the bluffs.

Matthew and I had left his house after picking him up, and after about three and a half hours on the road, we were pretty anxious to arrive, but also, we were a bit tired. In a moment, I decided to liven up the trip. I turned off the headlights as well as the dash lights. Initially, I thought it would give Matthew a thrill and a surge of adrenaline. I imagined I was just being that that crazy dad of his. I was always trying to be, what I thought, was a "cool" parent. Maybe I thought it would somehow make up for all the missed visits that I spent away all strung out or doing time in prison related to drugs. Well this ride certainly was memorable for Matthew and was later, understood, my own embarrassment for not being a responsible grown up. I had flipped the lights back on and exclaiming in tow "the battery came back to life, thank goodness." Matthew lit up like a Christmas tree, clearly excited.

Chapter 11

"We are made wise by the recollection of our past"

-George Earl Shaw

In the rural country, the sale of fireworks, of different caliber, such as: mortar ariel displays, and half sticks of dynamite make a party quite lively. I had been purchasing fireworks every time that I had an extra few bucks in my pocket.

On an occasion, that included Matthew's presence, we made the trip to spend the week with Randy. It was the Fourth of July weekend. I was loaded for bear by this time. Randy informed me that his cocker doodle, Charlie, and his pit bull, Zeus were no fans of fireworks. To be sure, he quoted, "They piss all over, bark at nothing, and hide in hard to reach areas."

I had purchased punks, which is a slow burning stick with a red hot ember at the tip, used for lighting fireworks instead of using a cigarette lighter. I lit two of them. It wasn't just the fourth of July; it was like Christmas to me because like most guys, I like things that go boom, and I was definitely going to share the wealth of adrenaline inflicted by the thunder from the explosions, and the stench of burning sulfur, bring to the senses. I brought Matthew to share in the experience.

I gave Matthew a punk and presented the smaller fireworks such as: smoke bombs, firecrackers and bottle rockets. He reacted just as I imagined he would. "Dad, let me light a big one!" He stammered. How do you say no to this kind of excitement? I said, "Okay just keep your head and body away from the launching tube, and if you think, you didn't light it , or you think it's a dud, stay back and let me handle it. The last thing we wanna do is get burnt." It had begun to rain steadily; this put no damper on our excitement. We must have lit $400 in fireworks in about an hour.

The dogs, Zeus and Charlie, did exactly as my brother, Randy, had warned. I ended up having to clean up urine and pick up overturned tables from the animals trying to escape the noise of explosion. Randy just shook his head at the sheer excitement Matthew and I displayed. He went on to remind us, it would be our chore, when morning shines, to track down all spent fireworks.

Chapter 12

"Man, never so often deceived, still watches for the arrival of the brother, who can hold him steady to a truth, until he can make it his own."

-Ralph Waldo Emerson

From living in the city, in constant drug activity, it was soon evident that my world was coming undone. I was heavily addicted top heroine. As most often, it starts with pills, but as you could set a clock by, they run out. Having interaction with multiple dealers, habits are, most often, easily maintained; but there comes a point where your delusion becomes your reality. Being awake and drugged for numerous days without sleep the grip you may once had with reality. Excessive use, of cocaine, can attribute, to paranoid idealizations, leading to erratic behavior.

Soon my own schizophrenic behavior had put a wedge between Julie and myself. It the drug world, it pays to be aware of ones surroundings. Robbery, at times resulting in death, is a constant threat. Instead of coming home, after deals were complete, I started renting hotels to conduct major drug deals. I often remained at the hotel for days, not even aware that I had not even checked in with Julie at home. Julie suggested that, I take a break and maybe spend some time up north with my brother.

After another couple of days, at a hotel, once again drugging myself, I grew quite delirious, to the point that I began to convince myself that a neighbor had plotted to rob and possibly kill me. The episode was so real to me that I made the call to 911 and begged law enforcement to help me.

"I don't want to die, please come quick." I begged to the 911 operator.

I could hear the sirens advancing closer. With every step of my running down the center of the divided highway, I waved my arms frantically, to be noticed.

The police rescued me, though there was no neighbor robbing or chasing me. They rescued me from myself. The officers took notice that I was, obviously, under the influence of something, most likely, illegal. I was soon searched and the motel key, offering where I was staying, was in my pocket, as well as a box cutter. At this point the officers placed me in the squad car and took me back to the hotel. Once there they searched my room for drugs. Thankfully, I had flushed the drugs down the toilet, prior, anticipating the search, before calling 911. At some point I went into a seizure.

I later became conscious in the area hospital. I would have to believe that the officers had made the circumstances of my situation clear with hospital staff, because, as I regained consciousness, I found myself strapped to a gurney. The muscle in my right calf seized with a spasm. Now restricted in movement, being in extreme pain from the spasm, the only thing the nurse would do is look at me and shake her head. I cussed and screamed from the pain of the spasm. I've come to terms; it most likely due to dehydration from not drinking water for days on end. Finally, after quit the scene I was making, another nurse came into the room with a syringe filled with liquid and injected the fluid into an IV that ran into a vein in my arm. I had no recollection of having the IV, pushing fluids, spiked into my arm, but with relief the drug the nurse injected did the trick and rendered me , once again, unconscious.

When I regained consciousness, I found myself in a hospital room, in which an aide was washing my hair with what seemed to be water less shampoo.

The hospital kept me for a number of days, as my body began to recover from the months of abuse I, myself, had done. I was visited by police officers, who informed me that there were to be no charges and that I was going to be released from the hospital, but I was barred and never to return to the hotel, by hotel owner's request.

Chapter 13

"They wish to be saved from the mischief of their vices, but not from their vices."

-Ralph Waldo Emerson

My brother, Randy, was soon attending various auctions in pursuit of vehicles, lawn care equipment, trailers and some heavy machinery to launch his dream, a landscape company.

After the hospital episode, I moved to the country with my brother, Randy. I left the truck with Julie as an excuse to come to city and, with hopes, to keep our relationship somewhat open. Randy tried to argue with me about leaving the truck, but I was love blind and put full belief this was only temporary and would soon follow suit by moving to the country to be again with me.

Randy made me an employee, because he needed the help and this was also a sure way to keep close tabs on me. Riding lawn maintenance equipment in the sun gave me a marvelous tan. Randy bought another work vehicle and gave me full access. You might say he was trying his best, to make good out of the situation.

I had to hand it to Randy; he had me covered on all basis. He had purchased a freezer bag of pills, an assortment of opiates. Soon pills coursed through my bloodstream firing mass amounts of dopamine through my brain. Randy stayed clear of opiates himself. I think, through his life, he had had enough experience with the physical addiction that came with continued use of opiates, but I found he surely enjoyed drinking vodka and orange juice by his makeshift bonfire pit. The arrangement was the base of an old Weber grill; for under town ordinance, the fire had to be "contained" due to the forest of trees that surrounded the area.

It wasn't long and still in contact with my friend Bobby, we made arrangements for him to visit. Bobby worked a factory job, but on his vacation time that he had saved up, so it became his plan, while on vacation visiting his friend, which was me of course; he could also make a couple bucks working with me and Randy with the business of landscaping.

After Randy and I picked up Bobby from the bus station, and we had been driving on the way back from the nearest city about forty miles away, fumbling around in the back seat, bobby fished a pipe and numerous individual bags of cocaine from his pocket. His next works were, "Anybody wanna get high with me?" He past the pipe up to me in the front seat and we engaged the rest of the trip home pleasantly intoxicated. After we had driven to Randy's trailer, Bobby pulled another larger bag of heroin from his other pocket. With this, all I could do was smile because this was exactly how I had known Bobby since I met him in jail for what seemed so long ago.

Randy left Bobby and I to our vices, but returned the next morning to pick us up to work. Bobby and I hadn't slept a wink but had painted the entire kitchen; and you could have eaten off the floor for we had scrubbed it, thoroughly. Randy could see how intoxicated we were, and opted out of allowing us to work with him that day, although he had a large land clearing job set up for the week. The next day, or was it two, Randy came back and this time we went off to work.

We had a system set up that required one person to saw the tree down, one to put the chains about it, one to pull the trees out of the clearing with the dump truck, and one to cut the trees to measured length. We had been working the job for a number of hours, when, as I was the one cutting the trees to size, the chainsaw bucked, and with a skid across the log and a nick or two up my pant leg, I gave a shrill yell. The chain saw had just skimmed my leg but had managed to take a little chunk here and a little cut there. I was done for the day, for Randy now found time to complain; he thought we were to intoxicated to work anyway. He may have been sore at us and with reason, but when after I loaded the measured logs with the skidster, being a small front end loader with a bucket to pick up heavy objects, Randy made his way, trailer stacked with logs, to the Amish man he had found to buy the black walnut.

Rand and I seemed to argue quite a bit; more so when I was high. A side effect of opiates is moodiness. He couldn't blame me for stupidity, though, when on route to the Amish, heavy with the weight of the load, he took an easier route but this route was up hill. Kicking the turbo in, transmission whining, he wore most of his clutch out before reaching the top of the hill. Now, Randy had reason to be upset, but it was no fault of mine, so I found it funny. I wonder sometimes why he even put up with me. I can only imagine, brotherly love.

Randy paid Bobby for the weeks he worked, and a friend of ours, Paul, whose mother lived in the same small town, helped Bobby in giving him a ride back to the city, rather than Bobby having to take the bus home.

Chapter 14

"Always kiss your child, even if they are asleep."

-Ace Jackson Brown Jr.

Now living up north, I still made trips to the city. I also did my best to spend time with Matthew. Randy, his uncle wished to instill in him the value of work, in which having his own business enabled him to give my kid a job. Ate the age of seven, Matthew worked with us. He would take part on the use of the weed wacker which was twice the size of him. He would soak up the details of the task as well as the encouragement randy would give him.

On one visit of the summer, which I had made the arrangements with his mother to stay for two months, Matthew brought his friend Cyrus. Randy had both of them come to give a hand at work. Working, I think, was a good excuse for Randy to give them money.

The job we were working on was to put in a patio of brick pavers. Putting pavers in, the foundation is of sand and a lot of it. The boys were in charge of filling the empty wheel barrels with sand from the bed of the dump truck, and I lugged the wheel barrels to the area of interest. Well as both boys were at work, somehow Cyrus smacked Matthew in the head with the shovel. And , of course, this brought worry of concussion. In turn, Matthew was ordered to sit in the cab of the truck by his uncle, my brother Randy hoping there wouldn't be a necessary trip to the hospital. Of course, Randy was still paying Matt for his time. Well, being a father of bribery feeling sorry for the kid, I fed Matt as much candy as he wanted with the daily allowance I kept on hand for myself, for I always had a sweet tooth. I had fed the flames of the sugar high and before long Matt began to complain of an upset stomach. Thinking back I seem to recall the four of us having food from the gas station for breakfast on the go. It was a good old soy breakfast.

It was soon apparent that a trip to the gas station was a need. The need, in particular, was the facilities, or more precise, the toilet. I felt bad for on the way, driving as fast as I can, Matt's next statement said it all, "I'm afraid to fart, dad." Looking to comfort his feelings, I retorted, "its okay I had to change my underwear before I came today, because I thought it was just a fart." I don't make it a habit to purposely lie to me son; this hadn't happened that day but Matt didn't know that. You would think that after this close call, for the event unfolded without a hitch, I would have learned my lesson long ago regarding candy, but there was sure to more to learn at a different episode.

As I have stated before, in boredom I found joy in art. It started with outlines and basic doodling. Then it was a compilation of accumulated pictures that I arranged to make my own idea of art. In search of a pass time that I had high hopes that Matthew would always remember; it was also just on principle that I wanted him to remember spending time with each other. We would paint together some scene of nature as to two grizzly bears fishing salmon out a white water river.

The paintings I had in mind had to be painted in layers. For instance water had several tones as well as the foam of which was to be presented- rapids. Matthew and I would take days on end in completing a single painting. It seemed to be fun for the both of us.

As was for sure to happen, in my absence, Julie began relations with another guy, but still came to the country to see me. I never doubted that she loved me but I suspect, the trips to see me were more about knowing that I always had pills, for working with my brother I had been introduced to another friend of his who had the connections for pills.

Regina, Randy's girlfriend, in having gone thru all he prescribed pain pills from the doctor, employed me to sustain her opioid dependence. This became lucrative for me, for in the country, I learned pills were worth double of what they are in the city. At least to her knowledge that was the given theory.

On one occasion, at some point, Julie came to visit for a couple days. When she decided that she was going to leave, I pulled a fast one and cut the wires to the alternator. I had known she had no study of the workings of electrical wirings or engines. As her plan, Julie left that evening on her return home. About an hour later, of course, my phone began to ring.

"Something is wrong with the truck," she complained. She informed to exactly where she was stranded. I headed on route like Prince Charming coming to save her. When I arrived, I charged the battery, reconnected the wires, and drove it home, as she followed in the work truck I had driven to rescue her. I had a couple more days to hang out with Julie.

On one morning, Randy took Julie and I out to breakfast at the bar/restaurant in town. After we ordered breakfast, Randy bought us each a scratch off lottery card in which I won two hundred and fifty dollars. I cashed it at the bar. This allotted me the funds to fix my "broken" vehicle. I drove it to the nearest station. In a cover up I lived the lie that the vehicle was having an alternator replaced. Julie would soon be back on her way home, as I still sat, incredibly, still in love with her. It sufficed me to know by observation, that she had no way in order to support her addiction. I knew that her own dependency would in all likelihood lead her right back to me. This time when she left the country there was no call of a broke down truck.

About a month later, having been working regularly with Randy in company of the mascot, Charlie, whose head was out the window, ears flapping in the breeze, Randy informed me he had plans to visit the city. As normal Randy rented a motel room and I went to visit Julie for the evening. Julie had company so I left; meeting up with Randy we cruised around the city that we had grown up in. We were real intoxicated, high as a kite, feeling no pain when we stopped by my old, and first love Lisa. Now mind you this is fifteen years after the fact. It is amazing that if and when one encounters a memory, a feeling of joy elevates your thoughts, but face to face some of those old feelings can twirl up your stomach and have you to feel those butterflies as you once did as a kid. We talked to Lisa's mother, nick named Squeaky, for she was a part of our past so long ago. I stammered and asked Lisa if she would like to go have a couple of drinks and maybe shoot some pool. She agreed, and I thought this was gonna be a hell of a night. We drove in her vehicle for I had left my truck at the motel earlier.

Randy had taken his vehicle separate; I mean it doesn't take much brains to entertain the idea that there stood a potential of a fireworks of a reunion between Lisa and myself, or so I thought.

Upon arriving at an alcohol serving establishment, Randy ordered the beer by the pitcher and made change to play a game or two of pool. Lisa and I played "catch up". I had met up with Lisa unexpectedly a year or so prior when , at the time, I was scoring some cocaine for Bobby, to find out , on a pit stop home, the drugs purchased were distributed at a tavern to one of Bobby's clients who happened to be, none other than Lisa. At that time, I merely said hello to Lisa in passing and no intent on conversation, for I was in need of a fix at that time and not up for accommodating small talk. This time it was different, or, so I imagined, this visit was gonna end on a much better note. Before two shakes of a stick, Randy informed me he was leaving and would see me later, for he would be at the hotel.

Lisa and I had a number of beers but after the second pitcher we decided to go and have a bite to eat. I think, it was a bit awkward, for we really had had no real contact in many years. We decided to head our way into a small town outside the city, for there was a small chain restaurant known for serving food late. But as crossed the bridge in direction of the diner; we neared the intended restaurant to find it vacant. Obviously, she hadn't been out to that diner for quite some time either.

As we circled the block, deciding where else we might go, the vehicle trailed us for about a block, and a nightmare soon unfolded. It was an unmarked Police car and before long he lit up his emergency lights in attempt to pull us over. When the officer excited his car and came to the driver's window, Lisa handed her driver's license out the window. The officer looked across the vehicle in time to ask me to supply some sort of identification. I obliged and passed him my identification. The officer spoke with Lisa briefly, but all I could think about were the pills in my pocket that I had no prescription for. My mind was busy calculating the milligram amount just in case I needed to eat them to avoid arrest after the search I just knew was about to take place. The officer returned to his vehicle to run Lisa's license and my identification.

When the officer returned, he appeared at my window and asked for me to step out of the vehicle. He asked if I had anything illegal on my person. Now I have gone through this so many times, I just assumed the position by turning my back and placed my hands on the vehicle. Without further ado the officer began his search of my person. He withdrew a pill bottle from my pocket and shook the bottle. I had nothing else but a bit of money in my pocket, so he ordered me to remain in the vehicle and he would be back shortly. After I got back into the car and secured the door, he returned to his car.

After skittish small talk between Lisa and me and what seemed like a long time as the moment lingered, the officer returned and asked Lisa to step out of the vehicle. The moved to the rear of the vehicle and with brief glances I understood that she was amidst doing a sobriety test which ended with her crying. A moment or two later she came back to seat in the car sobbing and I am sure the alcohol fed that fire of emotion and fear causing duress. I had no soothing words for her.

Next, the officer appeared at my door and opened it. I knew this was coming for harassment was second nature to law enforcement once they were informed of my background, of drug use, by way of that little computer in his car. The officer went on to explain that he had given Lisa a choice because she has no criminal record, but she was above the legal limit of alcohol consumption to legally drive a vehicle. He handed my pill bottle back not knowing I had replaced the pills with the illegal pills, or we would have been having a whole other conversation. He went on to say, "I know you're abusing your pills and I will be calling your doctor in the morning; for the pill count is incorrect. I've informed Lisa you are a bad influence and she will be going home so she can go to work in the morning. Where you go I don't care but get out of this town. Now you can start walking!" He handed me my identification and shut the vehicle door. Lisa drove off without a good-buy. The officer standing by his car went on to say, "Why you people need to prey on the innocent, I do not know. But you sure have a long walk ahead of you. If I see you in this town again, you will not be going home. "Long walk, "must have been referring to the address on my identification card, for it was three and a half hours' worth of a car ride. Thank God Randy answered his cell phone and immediately picked me up.

I tried to call that lost love of mine by the name of Lisa numerous times that day, then the next, and sporadically for the weeks to follow. I came to the realization she must have had caller identification on her phone and refused to answer. I can only say that maybe, some things are not meant to be, or just to stay the way they are for a greater plan. Although, for some unknown reason I think of her rather routinely, for which I will never truly know why.

Chapter 15

"Being able to accustom ourselves to some degree of physical pain, without immediately reaching for something to dull it, is an important life skill."

--Robert Greene

As what now has become a regular occurrence, Regina's call can be mapped with consistent accuracy; she wants pills, no matter how I come about them. Due to her recent inheritance, money not being a hindrance, if there are to be no pills found in the small town area, she would bribe me with a couple extra hundred dollars to take the three and a half hour trip to the city. As I had mentioned prior, besides the long drive this was a win-win for me, for the city held a significant price difference and pills were prevalent if you possessed the monies to buy them off the street. I began making the trip multiple times a week. Many time I told Regina there were no available pills in town, leaving the impression I had made the trip to the city inflating the price and impregnating my wallet.

When I did make the trip, I would spend time when I dropped in at Julie's apartment. I was missing sleep and still be to work with Randy by morning, often just getting back into town minutes before he arrived at the house.

Finally on one of these long trips after again stopping by Julie's, she informed me she wanted to move up north to live with me, for her "missed me." We packed up her apartment and put as much as we could in the truck. Over the next week or so we made several trips, filling the truck, unloading at the trailer until the trailer was filled with Julie's presence.

At some point, I have no idea when, we got a pet. The pet was this little orange kitten. Its name, simple enough, was "kitten". I am not quite sure who named it. It grew into a large tom cat. He like my habit grew quite large.

One morning, I awoke to a phone call from my sister, who lived in the suburbs near the city. She had been my Grandma Bette's aid for many years. It was one of those calls where, immediately hearing her voice, you can feel the dread travel the length of the telephone wire straight to your ear. The news: my grandmother had a tragic fall, hitting her head with such force that her brain had swollen, resulting in her death. Her walker remained near her bed, although knowing she had terrible vertigo, she refrained from using it. She died at the age of ninety-nine years old. She was my birth mother, Diane's mother. She had been a guiding angel top me all my life.

The next trip to the city was not for profit, but to convene at the funeral home, for a celebration of life. This was the same funeral, I had attended for the funeral of my great grandfather Herman, which by name alone seemed to me to be ancient. His son, my grandfather Harold had also been laid to rest. Now my grandmother Elizabeth would also share that plot of earth.

Grandma Bette's funeral was a time for the family to gather. Most of her friends had long ago on, as did all her immediate family, including her brothers and sisters. She had at one time explained that the worst part of getting old is that you get the chance to see everyone you care about die before you. I find comfort in what she had also once told me. She said, "I've seen enough and lived long enough, that though life is love, there is a time to let go."

She did have some old friends come to pay their respects. Burdened by the knowledge, of the life of addiction Randy and I had lived thus far, surely must have been the reason for the silent treatment given rather than condolence.

It is natural law, the past can never be changed and remorse does not change this.

The morning after the funeral the weather was twenty degrees below zero when we buried my grandmother next to her husband, next to both his parents and my own mother. There was one plot left in the graveyard, the land purchased for the intent to plant the bodies of the dead. I only wondered whether it would be me or my brother to fill that last open place. I expected it to most likely to be myself found knocking on death's door long before Randy.

Chapter 16

"The longing to commit madness stays with us throughout our lives. How is it that we hurt those we love, although we know remorse will follow? Our whole being is nothing but a fight against the dark forces within ourselves. To live is to war with the trolls in heart and soul. To write is to set in judgment of oneself."

--Henrik Ibsen

Regina's continuous calls, persistent in the desire to acquire the pills, never ceased until it became evident that she had begun to run low on money. However she had burnt through that once large amount of money can only be attributed to frivolous spending. Inconsolable, she began to sell her belongings. If Regina couldn't sell it see gave it away. This included: furniture, which she sold, her trailer which she gave to her niece after putting in a Jacuzzi as well as a remodeling to the whole interior.

My brother Randy had by this time put a major damper on their relationship when he realized Regina's pill addiction was also affecting he mental health. Realizing Regina was on a sinking ship, Randy bailed and moved out only adding to the downward spin of her mental health; he still was there for Regina as best he himself was capable.

When one notices someone selling or giving away their belongings, it is a sure sign of depression, but it also indicates that one may certainly be considering suicide. Of course, I had learned this through my own psychological process of that contemplation for many years throughout my life and recognized it, immediately. After pointing it out to Randy, whom also now recognized it, he did his best to remain in constant contact with Regina by way of the telephone, even while in the middle of hard labor.

I still received that expectant call, at the beginning of the month when she received her monthly, disability check. Through less trips of having to go to the city, for the drastically less and often absent amounts of money, Julie and I dampened our own addiction. We still maintained an addiction thru my working and a hustle of some sort was always in play. This included: trips to the city, doubling pill investments, distributing heroin and cocaine in the rural surrounding towns. I myself was up to my neck drowning in my own addiction.

With the final giveaway of her trailer, Regina decided she was going to go on a trip around the country in the only thing she had't given away, her truck. Regina having just acquired her own pain pills from her own doctor, she headed out and began her adventure! Randy stayed in contact even though Regina was taking more of the business' time than he could financially stand.

Regina trip seemed to end in Florida in which she rented another trailer, but she hadn't been a Floridian resident for a month, before Randy received the expectant call, that gave the picture of Regina's degraded mental health. She expressed, "She had seen an old adversary, who followed her all the way to Florida, put superglue in her locks, and while out shopping, plastered the walls of her newly, rented trailer with feces". It was obvious she hadn't been taking her medication, for she also had been diagnosed with paranoid schizophrenia. And added to the mental breakdown, I can only imagine, she was also in a terrible state of opiate withdrawal. Randy, empathetic, begged Regina to come back, offering his own trailer to stay in with Julie and myself until she felt better.

Regina accepted the offer and within a week or so returned, quite still in duress. She rarely came out of her room. Whenever I made a something to eat, I made her a plate to eat and brought it to her room. When she finally talked, she explained she had taken her only pain pills and she had been experiencing withdrawals, which would account for her isolation.

Julie was on social security and so the beginning of the month was for obvious reasons "a light in the darkness".

We made plans accordingly. When the first of the month came we were waiting patiently at the automated teller machine for the clock to read 12:01 am in which we could squander money for a trip to the city, with intentions: to visit Julie's family, purchase adamant amount of pills, and also to pick up my son, Matthew, to accommodate us to the trip to the country.

While at the family gathering of Julie's relatives, I made the appropriate phone calls to set up the purchase, which, at times, can take up to a couple of days to acquire verification of the needed product is available. We spent the night at Julie's families, and I gave Regina a call, for she wasn't in her room or present when we had left on our trip. The purpose of the call was to simply check on her well-being, but to also see if she was going to need my assistance in attaining enough pills needed to get her through the month in attempt to save an extra trip to the city. I sent numerous texts and left many voicemails implying the urgency needed, for I had a specific time schedule to arrive to pick up my son, Matthew, on the route back home. With no return call or text, we left the city heading to pick up my kid and travel home. Three and a half hours later we arrived back at the trailer. We unpacked and set in to relax from the trip.

I received a phone call from Randy. He was quite somber. He went on to inform me that he himself had come to check on things in the trailer earlier that day and had found Regina, thought to be passed out on the floor in her room in the trailer. Finding it odd for her to be sleeping on the floor in the middle of the day he straddled her and started to apply pressure in giving her a back massage. Gripping her by the shoulders he found her unusually stiff. It was the kind of stiff that seemed to have fuzzed her whole body. The realization and shock that overcame Randy that Regina was no longer among the living and left only the shell of her body behind slowly set in. He found her morphine bottle acquired through her prescription from her doctor, lying on the floor next to her, empty. Viewing the label, Randy informed us that it had been filled only two days before.

Randy went on to tell me he had called the emergency numbers 911 and explained what the circumstances he had stumbled upon.

Out of pure curiosity, I went to the room that Regina had died in to see the place where she had left her body behind. Though I happily was in no way responsible for her final act, but I couldn't help but feel terrible, for I had grown to like her as a person for all of her kindness and her obvious love for my brother. Upon further observation, I began to look at the trailer differently, due to my knowledge of police policy and procedure. I had no choice but to had accumulated the knowledge in dealing with the late death of my friend Kenny, not so long ago.

I could immediately feel as if something was pressing on my chest. There was present and in the wide open for anyone to see, blackened spoons which had been used in the process of liquefying pills inn the order o f being processed for injection into the blood stream also leaving a drug residue. I knew that this constituted evident paraphernalia in the residence which under a suspect death gave probable cause to the use of illicit, illegal drugs. Knowing this alone, I knew that the law enforcement was sure to be back with a warrant to search the residence.

Chapter 17

"Each night, we die a little death. So why do you continue to carry your woes? Awaken reborn."

--M. Lecher

After Julie, Matthew and myself had a couple of hours of sleep, I decided it the best course of action, to take Matt back home due to tragic death and the fact that it stood to reason and a good possibility, I felt, the police would definitely be returning to investigate further, probably with a search warrant. In all fairness I considered it to be completely in the realm of possibilities that law enforcement would ultimately just raid the trailer with high powered weapons dressed in combat gear. After, explaining only that Regina had died and the events to follow could be traumatic, not mentioning the police or possibly a task force raid, Stace, Matt's mother, explained that she had no plans and would be home if I chose to bring him back home, that she understood, and nothing further was said.

On the way home, it dawned on me that I had sent texts to Regina's phone regards to purchasing illicit drugs. I called Randy and asked him if he knew the whereabouts of Regina's cell phone. He went on to inform me that Regina's brother Greg had already stopped over and picked up Regina's personal belongings from the trailer which included her cell phone. I felt worry begin to creep in like a shadow from the sun.

The day passed without incident.

I received a call from a temporary service in which I had filled out an application at an earlier date for work through the winter months; for there was no work with Randy and the landscape company in the winter months. It was around noon that I began getting myself together, pulling on jeans, stuffing my face with a sandwich, when I heard an all too familiar pounding on the trailer door. Of course, it had to be the sheriff's department with, I imagined, a slew of officers. I answered the door to find a battalion of police brandishing a search warrant that stated direct and ado for the search of drug paraphernalia. After three hours, they had accumulated a shoe box full of syringes and blackened spoons. The spoons were blackened from the use of a lighter, heating the spoon to process the pill for injection, leaving a film of carbon caked to the bottom of the spoon. Also found were several cut straws used to snort crushed pills.

The head narcotics agent handcuffed me in the front of my body and took me to his police issued truck to interrogate me. He was all too well informed to have guessed what my regular routine and habits included. Obviously, it was evident from my past criminal record and in finding the box of paraphernalia that I have been an addict for many years, including the present.

The detective went on to inform me that Regina's nephew had called and spoke to the detective after hacking Regina's cell phone. He had later met with the detective to inform him by way of the phone that Regina had been purchasing pills and that there had been a conspiracy on my part to purchase pills for her. Interestingly, the texts that I had sent were sent, after she was already overdosed. This had been proven due to the learned fact in which the time of death had been confirmed and established prior by the county medical examiner.

I thought this was quite peculiar seeing that I myself had purchased a number of Ecstasy pills from him not two weeks earlier.

Due to the findings in the trailer, I confessed to the possession of the drug paraphernalia, for the was no reason for Julie or my brother Randy to also be held responsible when one confession would satisfy that long arm of the law. Due to the lack of sufficient evidence, having found no illegal drugs, there were no charges for any conspiracy to peddle drugs. The investigation into the death of Regina was now closed. I missed my first day of work.

After Randy bailed me out of jail, the following day I sought out help for my opiate addiction. I scheduled an appointment with a psychiatrist. At the appointment I bared my soul to the doctor and he placed me on the Suboxone program. Suboxone is a drug used in combating opiate addiction. It is a narcotic twice as powerful as morphine but as a unique ability to block certain receptors in the brain. This allows the addict to maintain life and function as others without the heavy sedation of heroine or other opiate derived pills. It is essentially trading one addiction for another. The doctor had me a on a very high amount of the drug so I began to cut down the amount I would take allowing me to squirrel away the rest. An addict knows when physically addicted the body doesn't function correctly without the drug. I cut myself down to a half a pill in the morning and a half a pill in the evening before bed. My prescription allowed me four pills a day. Before long I accumulated hundreds of pills.

Chapter 18

"Pain is also a joy. Curse is also a blessing. Night is also a sun. Go away or you will learn that sage is also a fool."

--Friedrich Nietzsche

Randy was living with a woman by the name of Lisa, and it was my understanding that Lisa's relationship prior to the relationship with my brother had been a physically abusive. Lisa's former boyfriend's name had been David. David and Lisa had been a couple when Randy had first moved to the rural country. In fact, they all moved up to the country from the city at the same time. The abuse between the two exacerbated when the two were using heavy drugs. The move to the country was an attempt to diminish their overindulgence in drugs.

Though David and Lisa's drug use had diminished once moving to the country, they soon replaced it with drinking large amounts of alcohol and the abuse continued. I had learned through drug rehabs I had been in attendance that the use of drugs is only the symptom of a deeper problem, just as a runny nose is the symptom of a cold. Well Randy, many days, had visited the couple to witness Lisa often had blackened eyes and also privy to a split lip. But when David went after Lisa with a chain saw, while being quite inebriated due to alcohol consumption, it was the last straw, and Lisa finally involved the police in fear for her life. A restraining order was filed and Dave, having no place else to go in the country, packed up and moved back to the drug infested city.

Lisa had served in the Army so she had a pension. Lisa then, also took a job in home care for an elderly couple. To all appearances, she was stable.

After Randy and Regina had separated, Lisa and Randy began seeing each other, and Randy had moved from his trailer into Lisa's apartment that was a couple of blocks from Randy's trailer that Julie and I rented from him for a small sum. Julie and I often visited the two of them for the we both needed sociability. We enjoyed each other's company for grilling and the consumption of beer. Even a dinner of crab legs and steak, prepared by myself at the trailer, we still seemed to find ourselves at the bar not long afterward.

I had been placed on probation by the order of the county judge. This was a severe consequence due to fact a death was involved on the premise; although toxicology confirmed Regina's death due to respiratory failure from an overdose of her prescribed morphine, my past drug history gave evidence to a continued problem I ultimately brought from the city into their county. With a big effort, Julie and I put a damper on the heavy drug addiction.

Randy would stop by the trailer bringing that extra cup of sugar or anything else I could beg, borrow or plead from him. He also would pick me up to go fishing or simply to take a pleasant ride through the country stopping for a bite here, a beer there and continued bonding being brothers and my best friend.

One day, Randy stopped by to talk. He informed me he was having severe money problems. I asked him how this could be having a business, working at a factory thru the winter, and also the income Lisa had coming in. He told me that Lisa had been sending her son large amounts of money to pay his bills, for he had lost his job. In doing so she had neglected her own bills. It also became quite evident her son was doing more than paying his bills. For an addict, the behavior is recognizable, clear as day. Lisa's son finally admitted to his mom that he had an opiate addiction that cost him at least a hundred dollars a day just to function.

Lisa started spending every free moment she had in the tavern drinking her into a stupor. She was also on psychiatric medication name Xanax, a heavy tranquilizer prescribed for her severe anxiety. She began using more than prescribed. She, also, was drinking heavy. This was known to be a deadly combination. In an inebriated state, Lisa would often black out, and often urinating in her clothes. Randy would, after working eight hours, find her at the tavern, and escort her home to be sure she made it home safely.

Lisa's loss of control grew steadily worse. Mixing the tranquilizers with alcohol, being a powerful combination, Lisa started losing control of her bowels without even noticing. Randy would find her in one of the two taverns in the town, guide her home, help her out of her clothes, wash her in the shower, and guide her to her bed. Then Randy would have to clean the bathroom of feces.

When in talking with Randy, we tried to find out how she was acquiring these powerful tranquilizers. He called to speak with her doctor in attempts to stop the abuse that Lisa was so blindly engaged in. She still obtained another prescription.

Having no choice, Randy still attended his temporary work at the factory located a number of towns over.

The one night Randy came home from work planning to change his work clothes, and head out to meet up with Lisa. Upon arrival at the house Randy found Lisa on the floor in the middle of the living room. He later told me he straddled her with intent of trying to arouse her from her stupor. She didn't appear to be breathing. Checking her neck for the rhythm of her heart, he came to the realization; Lisa was no longer among the living.

This was the second lady friend of Randy's that died of some sort of overdose in the last six months. The sheriffs investigated everything Randy told them of the steps leading to Lisa's death. This lead to the interviews of the bar owners of the town who collaborated Randy's statements of the time leading up to the death of Lisa. Lisa's deteriorating condition was noted and confirmed by each of the bar owners. It was also brought to light, Randy's continued efforts in attempt to help Lisa in her condition, being expressed by the bartenders. I could only believe Randy had done his best to preserve Lisa's life.

Chapter 19

"At the most we can do is make hysterical, unhappy people normally happy. We bring them back to the normally unhappy."

--Sigmund Freud

Regina first and Lisa second, their deaths wore heavy on Randy's soul. His own drinking escalated. He moved back in the trailer with Julie and me.

I was still working in a factory, the same factory Randy continued to work at, only on different schedule, for we had different shifts. He worked the day shift and I worked the night shift.

According to Julie, Randy started to spend most his free time on the computer, online; soon he came in contact with a friend whom we had both known since our teenage years, twenty years ago. Her name was Shelly. Shelly had married a close friend, also from the past, named Steve. Steve and Shelly had married young but had had several separations and this state of their marriage at this time. One day, Randy came home with Michelle in tow; he moved her in.

Charlie the cocker doodle, and Randy's company mascot soon acquired a friend when Randy and Shelly came home one day with a baby pit bull they named Zeus.

So as time would tell, in my opinion, Michelle is most capable of pure evil. Her attitude alone is destructive and always has been since her younger years. Yes, Michelle can be sweet as pie, but in the blink of an eye, she will turn on you and it is quite possible, she will stab you in the back. I'm not certain, whether she was just jealous of my own relationship with Randy, but she soon we were at odds.

I had been looking into online classes and decide to try my luck at taking a course in Building Construction Management. For the first couple of weeks I sailed right on through the courses until I started advanced mathematics. I struggled. I tried using the chat time with an instructor to guide me through. I found that learning online is more difficult, at least to me, than in house learning. I soon dropped out and gave up hope on that agenda.

Randy and Michelle were coming home to the trailer, every night, most often, inebriated. They would go to the taverns in town, for dinner, moments after Randy got home from work. Yea, but you see their dinners were definitely of the liquid variety.

Static was high in the trailer, and one night Randy come home hostile. I hadn't seen Randy like this since we were much younger and he would come home after drinking whisky. I rose to the occasion ready to once again battle. I realized after a couple moments in which he and I man handled each other that he was very inebriated and I am quite the advantage. I love my brother greatly and seeing the unfair advantage I had over him, I let him think he had won. It was evident that it was time for Julie and I to find a different place to live.

Julie, having a government check each month, for her disability, allowed us to save some cash to move. We sought an apartment, in the Capital so that I could get into study, in person classes, at the college in town. I immediately applied for the grants and government loans for the task. We found a small two bedroom apartment; it had a kitchen and a room one could make a bedroom. We paid a down payment and first month's rent to ensure our new address.

Knowing we were soon to move, it seemed, Randy became most unbearable and Shelly was just herself. If I could describe what she is like, I would say she has multiple personality disorder. I would never turn my back on her, don't believe a word she says, and never leave her in your house alone.

I think it set in on Randy that we were actually moving with or without his help, so he even help Julie and I move our things with the company trailer. We started off toward the Capital and Randy stopped, as was his routine on this road that lead to the city, and ordered burgers from the restaurant. He, of course, had brought both dogs along which he ordered them a burger each as well. That was a bad idea, After an hour or so driving the aroma in the truck was enough to gag on. We had brought "Kitten" Julie's tom cat, but he was in a animal carrier, not in the vehicle; but both dogs, that were in the vehicle, had severe gas from such rich and greasy food.

Of course moving to the Capitol was exciting, but we were certainly completely lost in the area. our next investment was a GPS navigation unit which we purchased from the superstore on Black Friday the day after Thanksgiving. After which, the store filled and cramped past capacity, the line for purchase of any amount of sales merchandise snaked throughout the main aisles of the store, this I vowed, no matter what the sale may be, the day after Thanksgiving, I would never try to enter, to purchase anything again.

I attended school and after a number of months I received thousands of dollar, the monies from the applied loans and Federal grants.

Due to my squirreling away of vast amounts of the anti-abuse opiates prescribed Suboxone, we were unable to abuse other pain medicine in the event we sought them out, due to the analgesic drug naloxone, which is the other active ingredient in the Suboxone, eliminating a possible intended abuse of opiates. Use of any other opiate with Suboxone brings in affect an immediate physical withdrawal. I find this is where there comes the understanding of being classed a "control substance".

Now as the nature of things, there came a day that the pills once again ran out. The sweating, cramping, headaches, a feeling to kick out some form of complete uncomfortable unsatisfied devil's urge out of the body, diarrhea, orneriness and the inability to function soon took the place of stability.

Seeing that the apartment floor we were living in was low income and we were sharing the bathroom, I I would purposely leave the Suboxone prescription bottle out. Of course, it was empty, but this left room for thought. Before long I got the bite I was looking for. A neighbor made a point to make conversation and as with any illicit street drugs, the banter of beating around the bush ensued. The next question was mine when I asked, "Do you know where to find any dog food?" This is street code for "heroin".

I was soon introduced to several people and it took a bit of money to find a supplier that I deemed to be worth the hassle to coordinate with. It first starts with having to deal with the addicts whose only motivation is to steal some of your dope. After a period of frivolously spending of quite a bit of money, you soon become known, for it is much like a community only made of users and suppliers. This is when like a gambler you put " all in". Of course now you are not going to allow your money to walk off trusting some drug addled brain to return with your product, so hence the introduction is made and now you have a supplier for all intent and purposes. There are many dangers for there are: people armed to rob and if desperate enough will shoot you; and then you have to consider the odds that you may be dealing with undercover law enforcement. This is what is known as "the game". With a background and criminal record, which is like having a college degree in the criminal underworld; after a deep dive is done to ensure you yourself are not law enforcement, the deal commences in the hours ahead.

As time passed, I soon had an increase in funds appear in my bank account from my grants and approved student loans, but as with having a connection, as such that I had, I had been fronted or loaned quite a bit of product from my supplier. It is much like fish in an aquarium, every day you have to feed them. This is the simplest example of the life of an addict and my heroin habit was now a gorilla. I guess I looked at it, when in dealing with fellow users; I wouldn't like to grow sick from not having the drug, so I in a sense feed my flock. The old saying rings so true, "birds of a feather flock together". I still lived with Julie quite comfortable.

Then one day Julie's son came to visit. It wasn't necessarily Julie and I that he came to visit; he had friends that lived in the city, not to mention it was the weekend of his twenty first birthdays. His name was Shane. Well Shane asked us to drive him to meet his friend. It was on a street right off the main street that I would pull to the curb. His friend soon pulled up in front of the car and Shane exited the vehicle with intent to only be a minute with his friend. I recognized his friend's vehicle and knew precisely what Shane was up to, for his friend was one of the cats I had had to interact with before finding a source with whom I finally had found someone favorable. I didn't say anything when Shane returned to the car. His first words were, "I didn't know you were dealing heroin". It had become common knowledge among the community I associated with that by reputation, I had enough for the average deal and the drug that I slang was of decent if not better than average. It also weighed in probation accurately to the dollar amount spent.

Shane managed to celebrate his birthday. Around midnight, I found him puking on the steps outside of the apartment. I basically had to carry his ass up the stairs to the apartment, in which he never left the floor, where I set him down that evening. Shane never went home, or better stated, he never returned to his prior residence. I would say he liked the city so much that he never left, but I am quite positive, he just wanted to keep getting high, for it after all was free for him and Julie.

One day during a purchase from my supplier, he gave me a sample of cocaine, and he told me to check it out and let him know what I thought of it. He went on to tell me that he had come across a quantity of the stuff and wish for me to distribute it. Before I left my parking spot, I filled my nose with it. Cocaine had been a demon of mine in my younger years, but I still enjoyed getting wired from the drug. I must have driven around aimlessly for the better part of an hour and then remembered quite well that the effects believing the drugs name should have been translated, "more". After the smallest amount of its use I always wanted more. I ended up calling my supplier back, re-meeting with him and then again made my way home.

I arrived back at the apartment, made a few calls and followed my dealer's actions and gave away each a sample, as he had done to me.

The phone became a nightmare. It constantly rang, for addicts rarely sleep , nor care at what time the call you. The phone was ringing endlessly. I eventually had to shut the ringer off in order to get some rest, but at times that didn't stop the few that knew where I lived from knocking at all hours on the door, more often than not, it seemed to have been the neighbors whom lived in the same building as us. It seemed it was also after a quick run to the store or a quick errand that upon return the pounding began.

The neighbors were brothers named Chad and Todd. Chad worked at a prominent coffee house chain. He was the manager there. He also made sure to work the drive through window. By doing so, he soon found it quite easy to do the adding of funds of service in his head. Knowing his paycheck was already owed to me, he decides to start skimming the till. Before long, I would get a call from him from work asking me to bring him a bit of product to the store. Driving thru the drive thru, he gave me a complimentary cappuccino and as change, usually, the amount owed for the product I bestowed upon him. He began embezzling hundreds of dollars a day. In my own mind, I suspected but thought it better not to ask either brother of as to their comings of the money.

I found it systematic that both brothers would be pounding on the door at a spell after midnight or even calling the phone so persistently I thought it would short circuit. Often even the phone didn't keep me awake any longer. Between school and keeping up with the jones, I was wearing myself to the bone.

Then one day I noticed he wasn't going to work. He finally told me he had been stealing the money from work. Both brothers soon packed their things and made their way back to their hometown in Michigan.

When in dealings of the sale of narcotics, one must trust your gut when it comes to the types of people one deals with, for there are all walks of life. Paranoia is not to be ignored, for I have learned your first instinct is the one to act upon. Your gut never lies, and it might save your life. It could also save you freedom from a client that happened to decide to fill in law enforcement on your activities perhaps getting himself out of a pickle due to his own arrest for possession of narcotics or any number of other felonies that one encounters in an addict's lifestyle.

By now I had an awful habit and still attending school. I would often find myself in the bathroom stall nodding out from a fix I had talked myself into needing during the last hour of class. Surely one can understand that learning new mathematics, in particular, is a struggle one can certainly associate with pain, mental pain. Well this was at least what I was telling myself for justification to do just a little more. My studies began failing, my direction in course lacking.

Not only were my studies lacking from being so high, but morning classes began to interfere with the morning rush heroin addicts are in upon waking. With supporting Julie, I and Shane's cocaine and heroin money was too tight to neglect what now was my first priority. This kind of life was beginning to be quite tiresome.

I was making use of client's vehicles to switch up routine. I met people at the gas station near the house or library nearby rather than having them come to the house.

I still made time to pick up Matthew and take him to the city. I would download movies and we would watch the latest releases. We would go on walks and bike rides through the bike trails that snaked around the city. At the bridge, we would watch the traffic of the interstate. It was a fight to be part of Matthew's life due to my addiction. It wasn't that I didn't want to spend every moment with him, for he himself was like a drug. He made me feel that I was worth something rather than the drug addict I knew I was. Watching him grow physically and mentally, I saw he, himself, had a big heart. I tried to make every time I saw him something special, but I failed miserably.

When he needed a jacket for winter, we made it plan to stop at the store to purchase him a work jacket he had his heart set on. When we finally made it thru the line and it was time to purchase it at the register, I realized I hadn't the amount needed. Yes, I had money but not the correct amount for the jacket he wanted. I was so ashamed. Matthew simply looked at me and said, "I don't need a jacket that bad, Dad". I knew he was lying but just trying to comfort his dad. Instead I made a rookie move and bought him a bunch of candy which he projectile vomited all of thru the living room, and all over the clean blankets like some poltergeist. I went without a blanket that night for it was too late to go to the Laundromat.

On occasion, I trekked to see my buddy Bobby. Nothing had change with Bobby's habits. We had made the trip in the snow. The trip which normally took forty-five minutes took an hour and a half just to get to Bobby's residence.

As long as I had known Bobby, he had always managed to keep a full time job, thus able to afford his drug habits. Bobby kept his drug dealer on speed dial. There were those times where he owed his dealer more than his paycheck. at these times I made myself available, this was one of those times. With a heavy addiction there is no such thing as functioning for work without the drug, so keeping Bobby with product was the best I could do for him.

Due to Bobby's lifestyle, often buying and selling drugs, he lived by the rule, "Anything you cannot leave in thirty seconds isn't worth having." This had Bobby always changing addresses on a regular basis.

We shot pool and had a good time hanging out with my friend. Bobby was real thankful for my help.

Deciding to get back before we got stranded for the evening, we headed out, back down the interstate. I drove at a speed I thought was safe till the tires caught a rut in the snow covered highway, and we started to spin. I was at least sober enough to counter the wheel, and we ended the spin in a forward direction, in which the car stalled for a moment. We had made a complete 360 degree circle. I managed to get the vehicle started and off on our way we went. We arrived home nearly three hours later thankfully safe and sound. We took rest in the apartment without further ado. The snow shoveling could wait until morning.

Chapter 20

"I wonder if this is how the Lord feels, able to see what foolishness men are up to, but canna do a bloody thing about it."

--Diana Gabaldon

Around the same time that Shane came and practically moved in, he would often leave for a night or so but this time when he came back he brought a pet to add to the clan. It just so happened that his sometime girlfriend was off to college and had no one to care for her pet ferret by the name of Tucker. She gave us the cage which includes his water bottle, hammock, some sort of tunnel, and his food dish. The cage was approximately four feet by four feet. He littered the floor of his cage with feces and that was about as close to potty trained as he was going to get.

Tucker was great fun, although while walking him, which included harboring him in a body harness, it was quite the task for he was so curious.

Out of the cage, he would rear up on his back legs to play while I wrestled him hands on. He loved to play with "Kitten" the tom cat, but that had proven to need close monitoring. It seemed Kitten was thinking more on the lines of lunch. It became necessary to keep them separated. Between the three of us, we were sure to let Tucker had as much time out of the cage as possible.

I was under the impression that surgery removes the scent glands when they neutered poor Tucker, but between kitten and Tucker the carpets kept odor quite specifics to pets. If it wasn't that tom cat spraying, it was Tuckers cage though I cleaned it every day. I even resorted to bathing Tucker regularly which he seemed to enjoy much like the radical act of a dog after a bath.

One day in particular stands out to me which turned out to be a "not so funny" matter. Julie's sister Deb stopped by to visit. Often I think she was just wishing to lay eyes on Julie, for Julie wore her state of mind on her sleeve. I think she also wanted to be sure Julie was taking care of herself. Well on this specific visit, after Julie and her sister returned from shopping together, kind of like private girl's time, with coffee cups from the coffee house in hand, they returned jubilant. Deb put her purse down to hang out a bit and that damn cat wandered over and sprayed on her purse. We were obviously quite embarrassed but what could we do; we had no excuse that held "water" this time. That was the last time, I think, Deb came to the apartment.

Chapter 21

"O' while you live, tell the truth and shame the Devil."

--William Shakespeare

Like most large cities, there is a program named The Needle Exchange. This is where volunteers drive to meet you by appointment to supply you with new syringes for the intravenous drug user. The program also supplies the anti-dote type medication called naloxone used to counteract a heroin overdose. You are required to sit down and watch a short presentation on the use of the lifesaving drug. There also stationary offices, such as Human Services, who also supply clean needles to the public to prevent the transfer of the H.I.V. virus. They also offer to administer a free testing for the H.I.V. virus.

I would often drive past the Human Services office on my way to school or on the way back from meeting someone. I was known in the office for I came for at least four boxes. Each box contained one hundred syringes. I was also supplied with a large red, bio-hazard, and plastic Sharps container.

I made a habit of supplying clients with new needles and would also give out the anti-dote for the others that sold heroin. In the event the event of an overdose this was often the difference between life and death. I needed to use it on others on several times, for often an addict thinks only of "the ultimate high".

Again, I had the perception that I was just a supplier to everyday people and that if it wasn't me, they would simply seek out the drug elsewhere. I don't condone the sale to pregnant women, children or the over indulged. The overindulged was a person who knew their limits but purposely did large amounts with no caution. The drugs themselves sell themselves. There is such a demand, that most often, as soon as you possess them they are already sold and accounted for.

Drug use often includes poor hygiene. This doesn't mean you don't take time to shower, but that you neglect the simple things like brushing your teethe on a consistent basis. Normal routines become broken due to lapses of time and days without sleep the repetition of normal activities become blurred, sometimes obsolete.

There are times when the supplier takes time out of his or her dealing routines. As a heroin addict and dealer one has to be prepared for the situation by always having an adequate supply of the drug for one's own habit. When own's stash gets low, it is absolutely necessary to set up a meet to resupply the product needs. On occasion, there are times when this doesn't always happen, hence the client's withdrawal ensues.

On one occasion, after multiple days without the amount needed for my regular use, I was well into withdrawal. I left my phone ringer on even though I had no good news for my clients. I had left it on in hopes that my supplier would return my call. I had located some of the product, but at this point, it was not my intention to dole it out for two reasons: it was definitely not the potency I was known for, the price was not compatible to the selling price I maintained. This latter meant it would take me to the red of my bottom line.

Julie took shifts with me tending to and monitoring the phone while each took a moment for rest. Rest was so needed. The kind of rest only sleep could provide, for we had been going without for so long due to the lifestyle we were living, often referred to as "life in the fast lane". On the fourth day without communication, the call from my source finally came in. It was 5:30AM.

"Hello", I answered. "Where the hell have you been?" I continued.

"Been out of town at a funeral of a family member," he retorted.

"Can we meet?" I asked with a plead in my voice. He knew I was hurting something fierce. I found it queer that he then asked, "How much do you got?" I'm sure he realized that I was gonna be short on the monies that I owed having to care for mine, Julie's, and Shane's habit for four days. He never cared before exactly how much I had, for I somehow always had a large bill with him. He gave me a destination which varied between four regular different spots on any given day. We set the meet.

The first of the obstacles was completed.

My ability to use other people's vehicles was convenient due to the fact earlier by a month, when a morning before school, I I preformed my normal routine of warming the car for my voyage to the campus. One particular morning, the engine compartment starting broadcasting a noise that I knew could not be a good sign. I called the shop and they came to pick it up. But before the driver of the tow truck left, after a quick inspection, he told me that it sounded as if the bearings of the ballast register were shot. I had no idea what this meant, but after he got it to the shop, about an hour later I was informed by phone that the bearings were shot and my best option was to scrap it, for it would cost too much to fix. At this point, we were now without a vehicle.

I was able to contact the neighbor that regularly allowed me to use her practically new car for a bit of help with her own habit.

Snow surrounded her car. Still fatigued from withdrawal, ornery from blowing my own car's engine, and without getting much sleep, I used the brush enough to clear the front windshield and slid into the front seat throwing the snow scraper behind the passenger seat.

I really paid no heed for it seemed the car made its way, being front wheel drive, down the street. When the road ran out, for it was a left turn only, I braked pumping the peddle to take the left turn. Instead of stopping or slowing down, the vehicle started to slide and no matter what I tried to do, I was moving too fast to avoid the curb ahead. You would think I had never driven in the snow, for I surely should not have tried to drive at a speed not aware of the road conditions.

The steering wheel turned, the car still advanced forward. My only thought, at this point, was to try and save my neighbor's front end alignment of her car by hitting the curb with wheels aimed forward, rather than sideways resulting in twisting the front end, possibly the frame of the vehicle. I hit the curb, scraped the ground effects that gave the car its sporty looks, and knocked out my front tooth when I made contact with the steering wheel with my face, because I had not been wearing my seat belt.

My mouth felt like someone had punched me awfully hard in the face. Remember I had mentioned that bit about poor hygiene? I'm sure that had a bit to do with my tooth breaking off leaving the root and the other half left sticking into the steering wheel. At this point blood was a steady flow filling my mouth to overflow down my chin onto my shirt.

I backed the car off the curb hearing the plastic grinding on the cement as I freed it from its anchor on the cement. I got out the vehicle to find that the riveting had pulled loose. I picked it out of the snow and place in the backseat of the vehicle. I found the front quarter panel creased with an indent, but reached behind it, with a bit of pressure, surprisingly, popped it back in place.

I met with the source twenty five minutes later. Deal done I steered the car carefully down a side street and pulled up to the curb and stopped. Before I pulled the car away back into the flow, I injected a bit of the drug in attempt to cease the withdrawal that plagued my body. With a quick fix the pain melted away and relief set in. It was as if someone had suddenly poured a warm bucket of love over my weary soul.

Accidents are inevitable with the amount of drivers on the road these days. And let me not be misunderstood, as with any drug prescribed or street drug, when the effects hinder one's ability to drive, it is definitely careless, as with excessive speed is rightly so. I find it a fine line between medicated and over indulgence.

Carelessness is a demon.

Same car, different trip, the sun was yet high in the Sky; thankfully so, for the sun across the horizon can be quite blinding. Plunging forward, I have found myself leading the car only by the lines much like on a country road with oncoming traffic and their blinding headlights. This was not one of those days, for the sun was high in the afternoon.

It was a good day.

I was driving the five speed manual transmission winding out the gears. Newer vehicle the gears hitting home like a warm knife through butter. Music coming thru the speakers and the windows down, for it was beautiful weather. But there are always some idiots on the road. This day it was the operator of a motorcycle, better stated, a crotch rocket. He revved out the bike and brought it up to speeds of sixty miles an hour, then back down as low as twenty five in a zone of forty five. I cursed him as I safely passed him, sick of his shenanigans.

I shot up the highway in route to my meet. Feeling alright, elated, I maneuvered the five speed, switching gears as would one in a race car. The weather was warm; I slowed for my turn and downshifted. I rounded the corner and punched the gas. I was a block away from the meet.

A city block and a half down the road, there is a tee where there is an intersection. My normal parking space is facing east and I am driving west. At the tee, I slowed and down shifted to make the U-turn. I checked the mirror and saw a cyclist turn the corner still a block and a half behind me. I have time for the U-turn. My attention went into my turn. I was slow and deliberate for I was pressing redial on the phone, contacting my source in attempt to aware him I was at the meet. Everything became slow motion.

The cyclist could only have hit the gas immediately following his turn. I saw him too late. It was his acceleration that caused the catastrophe as he nailed the front quarter panel of car. He flew off the cycle onto the hood of the car. He then slid off the hood onto the pavement.

I jumped out of the car and heard him moaning on the ground. He didn't seem to thrilled when I went to my trunk and grabbed a blanket and tried to cover him with it. If all the police profiles are right when one covers a body it is the psychology of one's guilt, then I must have felt guilty, but the only thing that seemed real to me was the dent in the front quarter panel of my borrowed car.

My source drove by in his Cadillac, obviously, not stopping, for a police cruiser had just pulled up to respond to the accident called in by someone in the neighborhood.

I gave out the insurance card I found in the glove compartment and made the dreaded call to the vehicles owner. Relief poured over me when her first reaction was, "are you alright?" The state of her car didn't seem to matter as much as to my well-being. Thank God for insurance.

After the motorcycle was put on the tow truck, for the front end was in need of repair, the police left the scene and I called the source again and made the meet as previously planned without a hitch.

Chapter 22

"Speak of progress as much as you want. Even when you take out the canines of a tiger and he can only eat gruel, his heart remains that of a carnivore."

--Gustave Flaubert

Cocaine. The initial release of dopamine in the brain stimulates the user to great heights; but asks anyone that has used cocaine and they will agree: to use it once your desire for more overpowers any morals or virtue one values. Prolonged use of the drug causes paranoid schizophrenia. The power of the drug can take anything you value from you, material or mental. Cocaine is expensive due to the illegal trade and the plants used to make the drug can only be cultivated in tropical climate and is an illegal import.

Due to the desire to ingest the drug constantly while under the influence is what "rips the carpet from under your feet," so to speak.

My use of the drug began to eat the profits from the sale of heroin. And now to compound the problem by also supplying Julie and her son Shane daily doses of heroin, but now the added cocaine use which I provided free of charge, the bottom line was falling in the negative. Worse yet when an addict uses a stimulant such as cocaine, it speeds your metabolism. This in turn doubles the amount of heroin needed to circulate through your system to avoid the physical symptoms of withdrawal. By now that monkey on each of our backs had turned into a gorilla and it seemed to be my responsibility to sustain all of us. This cost was in the ballpark of three-hundred and fifty dollars a day. I started dealing in smaller quantities to maximize profits. This comes with greater legal risk.

As stated the loss of mental capacity is onset by continual use of cocaine. When you add this to the burden of any person already dealing with mental illness, it is sure to compound the problem greatly. I should also add that due to living on the precipice, greatly under the influence of hard core, heavy, drugs, by nature, you are not going to keep up with even the simplest of responsibilities.

By this time, it was no shock that I was failing three of my seven classes in my college curriculum. Between the missing days from much needed sleep and classes missed when I fell asleep in class or in the bathroom stall, I had lost any edge I once had. In the strict meaning of the word "intelligence", I was failing miserably.

Julie's mental health was also in crisis. Her stability, once given by scheduled medication, was lost. She began to believe that the neighbors had drilled holes through the walls to watch and spy on us. She began screaming outbursts directed towards the wall and personal attacks on the neighbors. I took her with me as much as possible in attempt to get her out of the house and into fresh air. She became hysterical, often believing we were followed or participants in a official drug sting by a task force. There came a point where my eating habits diminished, but Julie refused to eat anything and quit taking her medication for her mental illness all together.

At times, I couldn't take Julie to meet with the source; and these meetings often took extended periods of time due to the quantity of product I was obtaining for distribution. Julie would take walks, but on one occasion I received a worried call from Shane informing me that Julie ad been gone for hours and she had not taken her own coat. It being the middle of winter gave much cause for concern. Most times she would return home without incident, but this time I soon got a call from a local hospital. She had been found on a bus stop bench unconscious. Someone had called an ambulance. She was lucky to not have gotten frostbite on exposed members.

During this same incident, Julie spoke with the mental health official at the hospital and after the interview and her parents informed of her failing mental health, she agreed to stay for a couple of days in the hospital to get back on her mental health medications with the goal of mental stability. Her mother drove an hour to be present at the hospital. I think it was in concern for Julie, but it all went to hell when the hospital denied her ability to stay due to a drug test exposing heroin and cocaine use. I found out that those are two issues, mental health and drug abuse, are not to be remedied at the same time, but in due course separately. Julie returned home with me after her mother nearly assaulted me in the hospital.

I was now hated by her parents, for I imagine it was easier to blame me for Julie's choices. Although, Julie surely wouldn't have had such access to the amounts of heavy narcotics she was using due to my affiliations. I understood it perfectly.

Shane's heavy us, instigated by my resource, also attacked his own mental health stability. Hard core street drugs may take you high, but what goes up must come down, just like the law of gravity. So Shane was in a fit of depression, deep depression. Beside the drug abuse issues, he suffered abuse, the family kind. He had a hard time keeping work, an added pressure. Cocaine ripped the rug from under him. Shane reached out to his grandparents, Julie's folks. Shane bled out his secrets and the shit was piling up. He called his father, a recovering alcoholic, and grabbed his empathy, for Shane's past drug behavior and conduct associated with his past had been evident in his mental deterioration before his visit to my world His family got together and made a plan for Shane's recovery by way of rehab.

Shane agreed for the plan of drug rehabilitation and the date was set. When the day arrived he tried to back out. The worry of the physical withdrawal is a scary idea to contend with, but it is the first step towards recovering your life before the drugs had taken over. Julie, his mother, was quite aware that her family was concerned for Shane's well-being. She put her foot down and gave him the tough love needed, hoping for him to choose a better future. Shane's father came the hour drive to pick him up and drive him to the rehab facility.

I knew from this day forward that if there ever came a time that I would communicate with Shane again, there would be a very negative attitude towards me. I knew he would blame me for the choices he and his mother made in using the drugs that will and can always be depended upon to wreak havoc even on the sanest of person's life.

Chapter 23

"Men will only become better when you make him see what he is like."

--Anton Chekhov

When dealing with wit heroin addicts, as their supplier, it is good business to supply the addict a dose usually mid-morning, regardless if they have money to pay for the product or not. The reason being that a heroin addict needs his fix to function. If the client is not functioning there is no way to expect any profit from the individual. So by giving him or her their morning fix, not only does the client resume business later in the day, but it gives them the feeling that you have compassion for their situation and the proverbial tie is bound.

A client of mine called one morning as was his regular routine. His name was Doug. Well as normal Doug has no money this morning. This was expected for he is also addicted to the cocaine that I also supply him with. Cocaine can be expected to have you sell all your material belongings and quite possibly your soul, so it is expected for Doug to be broke, for he spent any and all hopes of money the night before. I explained to Doug that I was just leaving the house to tend to some errands and that I would call him when I was in the vicinity of his neighborhood and we would then meet.

It was a Saturday and I had no classes so on my way out I put a small package together to ensure Doug's worth to me for another episode of his use.

I jumped in the car and headed towards Doug's father's home, for that is with whom he resided along with his girlfriend.

There are certain routines one can do to ensure one's freedom which is always in jeopardy in this lifestyle, for remember this business is illegal and very well could be a free trip to a long incarceration. One of my routines is to never be on time and always unexpected, which is meant to complicate a possible law enforcement sting operation. So on this day, as I rounded the block of Doug's place, I noticed an unmarked police vehicle. Unmarked referring to the vehicle not having the emergency lights mounted to the roof of the vehicle. I noticed the vehicle being law enforcement from spotting the emergency hazard lights that were mounted to the back window. Now remember, I told Doug that I would call when I left the house and was on my way, which I did not do. I continued to drive and rounded the corner of the next block up from Doug's place and pulled in a auto dealership as i punched in Doug's phone digits. I had gotten out of the car and made my way to his door. I told him wait outside. So when he went out to wait, I was standing on his porch to meet him unexpected. I handed him his package and informed him of the law enforcement parked up the block. I waited for no reply and was gone as fast as I had arrived.

Note to memory: Doug may be compromised.

Later in the evening Doug called, for I knew he would and I told him I would pick him up from his house. Julie came along with me for the ride. We stopped for fried chicken in route to the meet for I had a hankering for chicken.

Not wanting to discuss business in detail across the waves of a cell phone that can anytime be monitored, I would pre-package baggies of product, cocaine or heroin for the purpose of quick and easy distribution. When in the dealing of the sales of illegal narcotics, in which I was up to my neck in, your first instinct of your gut is a force to pay attention to and heed. Although paranoia is a side effect of drug use, if heeded, it can also save your ass. To heed your paranoia is to save yourself loss of freedom or even save your life, for to live lawless is to live among the lawless.

We picked up Doug from his home after circling the block to be sure this time there were no law enforcement vehicles parked in the vicinity. Doug had less than a hundred bucks to spend informing me that he was getting it for someone else. I am known to drive fast, for it is the only way to see if someone is following you. So as I cut some corners we came to rest at a curbside for the transaction. No one seemed to have been following us for the street seemed empty.

I flipped on the interior light to see what I was doing and pulled a bag from my pocket and a cosmetic mirror from under the driver's seat. My thought being to share a line of coke among-st us three being: Julie, myself and Doug. I handed Doug a bag for his worth and passed the mirror around for the substance ingestion.

As I twisted the bag of product, in attempts to try and put in back into my pocket, someone rapped on the passenger side window, startling me. A bright light shown into the car. This was either an attempted robbery or an attempted police contact was the first things that crossed my mind. Either one, I wanted no [part in. The vehicle was running so I put the manual transmission into gear, turned the front wheels towards the street, dumped the clutch, and punched the gas pedal propelling us forward into the street.

I heard, "Stop! Police!" But then at the same moment I felt the car seem to bump something or someone on the driver's side. At a further glance, I saw what appeared as if I had just hit a police officer with the car, who apparently had been standing at the driver's side door. My minds only thought was the tally of police charges that I knew to be racking up. In a moment I weighed my options and imagined the chase that would ensue if I continued on the path I was headed in. Hitting the police officer with the car could very well be a charge of attempted homicide of a law enforcement official, and a high speed chase would bring added charges along with the fact that in a chase the criminal was most likely caught, for you cannot out run a radio signal, which is used in law enforcement to communicate with a whole fleet of other police officials.

I hit the brake and chose to stop the vehicle.

Because I make it a habit to lock the doors, the driver's side door was locked, which gave me an extra second to decide what to do with the bag of drugs still not made it to my pocket. The knotted bag had four, fifty dollar bags of heroin, and almost a quarter ounce, being seven grams of cocaine. The police officer is pulling the handle trying to open the door, which was locked; and as I witnessed the officer pulling his baton from his belt, which I knew his next act was to break the window, I shoved the bag of drugs into my mouth.

I tried to swallow the bag of illegal drugs, but had very little spittle in my mouth due to severe dehydration. I was unable to swallow. I was panicking. I accumulated a bit of saliva; I hoped it was enough. I swallowed and the knot of drugs stuck in my windpipe obstructing my access to air. I could not breathe.

The police officer struck the window with his club. He grabbed me by the coat pulling me through where once a window was. I tried reaching up to dig my fingers down my throat so I could get a breath. The officer threw me to the ground and grabbed both my arms pulling them behind me. I couldn't speak. I struggled thrashing about. The world of a white winter turned black as I lost consciousness.

When my sight returned, I realized I was in a confined area with three adults around me in the tight quarters. The man closest held a sopping plastic ball and reported, "Got you back!" As the realization that I was in the back of an ambulance set in, and knowing the sopping plastic glob in the man's hand was my bag of drugs, that I had tried to swallow and he had obviously retrieved it from my throat, the gravity of the situation set in.

This came almost as a relief, for in living this life of lawlessness in order to supply my habit and those around me, It was such a struggle to maintain any semblance of sanity. The constant threat of the loss of freedom if happenstance I was to run aground into it with law enforcement, the knowledge of robbery by any of the type that I surrounded myself with, and trying to satisfy the pusher, had all taken me to a precipice.

When I was cleared, after a visit to the hospital to be sure I sustained no injury from the fiasco, I was ushered to the county jail to be booked in for my alleged crimes. In the process of booking, I was taken to a nurse to be asked questions regarding my physical and mental health. One question is always asked in every booking. "Do you have any thoughts of hurting yourself or others?" was the one question that shook me to the core. Now, of course, I would have liked to have gotten my hands on Doug, for he surely had something to do with the situation I was in. Then considering the pain of physical withdrawal I was about to feel, along with the comprehension I was surely on my way back to prison for an extensive stay, I replied, "Right about now I wish I could die!" This was the wrong thing to say, for in jail this is as good as a threat and now the nurse hit an emergency button at some convenience. Before I could say, "oh shit", I was surrounded by officers and was physically stripped of my clothes and given a what is called a turtle suit. It is a stiff, flame resistant type of quilt that fits with Velcro around you like a barrel, naked underneath. I was tossed in a cell with a bench and a toilet and every couple of hours a nurse would open the door of a small window on the cell door to peek in on me. She must have seen me shaking as the withdrawal began to set in, for she opened the door to hand me a stiff five foot blanket, the type you use in a moving truck. There were no precautions not taken regarding self-harm, for I was under constant surveillance from a mounted camera in the corner of the ceiling of my new residence, the jail cell.

For the next three days, I made much use of the cold, stainless steel toilet, as I violently voided the drugs from my system from every poor and orifice of my body.

Chapter 24

"The truth is always pure but never simple."

--Oscar Wilde

Embarrassing isn't even the word to describe how I felt when the bailiff of the sheriff's department ushered me into the courtroom for a hearing on the likelihood of my release on bail. And it was sure my luck that the courtroom was filled with spectators either reporters or others and possibly their family members for support of their own court cases set on this particular date. Dignity was lost as I plead "not guilty" to the charges of possession of a controlled substance with intent to distribute, and reckless endangerment by use of a motor vehicle.

The reporters were in attendance for my case, for my arrest had made the newspaper as well as the nightly news. Apparently, I had been the subject of an ongoing investigation for several months by the drug task force. The regular routine of investigation had been lacking for the task force was unable to track me by usual mode of a GPS tracking device for, myself included, the car of my use was never consistent. My lifelong appendage of drug use, leading to the business of dealing the product, had rendered me the skills of avoidance by random movement, on offensive language skills in the direct communication in the order of the delivery of the substance, and sheer paranoia had allowed me the ability to elude the traps set by law enforcement. Law enforcement got their licks in as I was devastated when the cameras in the court showed me in nothing but a turtle suite for all to see on the evening news.

Still in custody, I served with a warrant, for all things, failure to pay child support. In my fast lane of a lifestyle, I had failed to send any monies for the care of my son. I hadn't even sent in ten dollars in the period of one hundred and twenty days.

The choices I had been making, without second thought, hadn't only taken my freedom, but would without a doubt steal me away from a relationship with my son. The years sloppily put into an education would also be lost, for I was sure to miss my finals for the semester.

While sitting months as my court case and attorney visits passed slowly by, I was able to call Matthew on the jail telephone. I had decided that he was old enough to tell the reasons for my constant absence in his life by way of jails and prisons. I called him and told him I got in trouble with the law again and was in jail and that I wanted to tell him why this "is". I went on to explain that I was a drug addict, which meant that I was addicted to drugs. I nearly reeled in shock when he replied, "I know dad, I looked under the door at Uncle Randy's when I came to visit and I saw you with a needle, poking it in your arm." My heart sank with sadness. No child should have to see or be exposed to something so tragic.

I plead guilty to the crime of "Possession of a controlled substance (cocaine) with the intent to deliver" and all other charges were dismissed, for the officer that I had hit with the vehicle during the arrest informed the district attorney that he was quite sure that I had not intentionally tried to run him down in the street. I have no idea why the charges for the possession of heroin were dismissed. Doug had signed a written statement that I had indeed sold him a quantity of cocaine the night of the arrest. I was sentenced to two years in the state prison and four years of supervision following the time spent in prison. If I were to continue and get caught for any other criminal behavior I could be re sentenced for up to ten years to be spent in prison.

I also plead guilty to "Failure to support a child", in which the judge sentenced me to two more years in prison, but made the time to be sat in prison during the same time spent as my drug charges. I will never understand why a prison sentence is given for child support; for how ever will one maintain a relationship with the child, let alone help financially, if left to rotting in prison. All things considered, I had dodged a bullet, so to speak. For all intent, I need to dry out from the heavy drug use anyway.

Chapter 25

"When sorrows come they come not as single spies, but as battalions."

--William Shakespeare

I, myself, really hadn't had very many that I would call friends. Surely, there were many that I would call acquaintances, yet even those I would consider only "passer byes". And certainly to consider the clients that I sold drugs to t be friends would be a mistake.

Bobby, however, was, in my book, a great friend of mine. Through the years, after meeting him through the jail experience, we had both helped each other out through a couple of hard times. No matter what was going on, we were always in touch with each other. Though we were both addicts and at times quite poisonous for each other, on that level, through life's emotional turmoil, I never not thought of calling Bobby to unload emotional struggles or problems.

Bobby had found himself in some legal trouble as well. He had been arrested and charged with possession of heroin and after living a life associated with criminal behavior, having had multiple run ins with the law, knowing how the judicial system functioned, Bobby volunteered for course of treatment to minimize his exposure to a possible lengthy prison sentence. He placed himself and was accepted in a drug treatment utilizing the drug called Vitriol. It is a drug that is injected into a muscle of the body by a physician. It is saturated in the system of the body and brain blocking the opioid receptors. In doing so, the addict is unable to feel the effects or high that accompanies the use of heroin. Once taken the injection of the drug lasts for a period of a couple months.

Bobby also complied with the counseling suggested by the program director.

When the date became close to sentencing, I knew that Bobby was itching to uses for from my calls from prison we talked about it on several occasions. Bobby even had mentioned that he believed the effects of Vitriol were suspended because he was do for another injection, for months had passed by since his first injection of the drug.

I wrote Bobby from my prison cell. Bobby was one of the very few people that kept up with me even though I wasn't out in the free world with him. Hell or high water, Bobby and I kept communication lines open.

Most friends, acquaintances, and even family are so caught up in their own life; they don't bother finding time for someone in prison. I have even been told by others, "I didn't put you there; don't get mad at me for not writing." My reply was, "Hey no matter if I'm across the city, on vacation in another state, or driving the car, I still keep up with you. So what is the difference if I'm in prison?"

I received a letter several weeks later from Bobby's mother. His mother knew me well, for she knew Bobby and I were thick as thieves. After reading the first couple of lines of the letter, tears from my eyes began to roll down my face. My close friend Bobby had died a week prior of an overdose of heroin.

Chapter 26

"The course of true love never did run smooth."

--William Shakespeare

I had proposed to Julie, for marriage, two months before my arrest. It happened that that year was to be a leap year. So our plan was to marry on the twenty-ninth of February. We thought it would certainly show to be a special day for a marriage. The marriage never happened, for I was certainly being held against my will, and would be for quite some time to follow.

Few relationships between man and woman last while either party is incarcerated. Through my experience, I marked notice that the relationships will often last half the total amount of time spent in a committed relationship. This is simply saying, your relationship after incarceration will only hold together so long; for a relationship five years old will only last two and a half years longer with the best of luck.

After my arrest Julie's family came to the city to rescue her. Julie had wrestled the heroin and cocaine addiction I had ultimately left her with. Julie informed me that a mutual acquaintance had supplied her with small amounts of the drug, in which she was able to wean her physically dependent habit down in increments, until the withdrawal was tolerable. She then was able to move in with her parents to rebuild and restore her mental health.

Due to lack of transportation, Julie, living in the suburbs with her parents was unable to come to jail to visit me. Soon I was transported across the state for evaluation and placement in the state prison system. I didn't see Julie for over a year.

Julie and I corresponded with written letters through the mail. Julie paid in advance for the much needed collect, telephone calls, which were much needed. Our relationship was stable.

Julie fully supported me during my incarceration. This included: Sending me the cash amount of fifty dollars a month, for such thing as candy, coffee, chips among other edible; she purchased a television, headphones, a guitar, and radio and sent them to me. She soon was on my visiting list and visited usually every three months when she could acquire a driver to bring her, whom she met in the recovery group, where she spent most her time. Every time I would call she was there to lift my spirits.

As Julie's mental health began to improve and she regained some stability, she was soon able to move into her own apartment back out on her own. Julie's family fully supported her efforts by driving her to appointments, grocery shopping, and her sister would take her out for coffee a couple of times a week, just to be sure she had something to do. Her family supported her in every way except when it came to anything to do with me.

In conversation with Julie, on the telephone, she would often discuss the sobriety club where I had met her, where she frequented, and talk about the people that still frequented the joint. A name kept coming up. The name was David. Now, David was an acquaintance, Julie had known, when I had first come onto Julie, years before, at

143

that same sobriety club while I was yet in drug rehab. David was a severe alcoholic and often came to the club drunk even though this was frowned upon. Julie had expressed, in those days past, that David made her uncomfortable. His casual flirting had often come down to straight forward, often belligerent, one liner. There were repetitive sexual advances and innuendo wasn't beyond approach with David.

Towards the end of my sentence of confinement, near the last two months, it seemed to become an issue to ever get a hold of Julie by telephone. I soon began to suspect that though she had been with me through this peril time, her entanglements with a possible some other were making themselves known. It seemed that if and when I did get a hold of her, there was an elephant in the room.

My release day had finally come. In corrections, it is common upon release to be placed back into the city of the transgression. I was placed in the county of my case of child support. Probation and parole had set me up in a transitional housing unit, specifically for those whom have no address to live at. Julie had not given me permission to list her address, so I was unable to list her address as my own on my release plan.

When I got off the bus, I had fifteen dollars in my pocket and three boxes of junk I had accumulated while in the joint. Expecting to be picked up from the bus station, to be transported to the temporary living home, by my parole agent, I was greatly mistaken and had to take a cab to the parole office across town.

After formalities of laying down the rules, my agent then drove me to my new residence. As we pulled to the curb in front of the apartment, all I could do was to shake my head.

We were in the inner city and my fears were soon confirmed that this living unit that I was expected to stay at was situated between two twenty four hour drug distribution houses.

Whatever government program that funded this fiasco supplied me with two ten packs of hot dogs, processed cheese, and two loaves of bread. This was all the help I was gonna get and was expected to integrate back into society.

After finally reaching Julie by telephone, I took a number of buses, for she had moved to a moderately populated city. However, I didn't happen to find her apartment easily. After getting off at the stop she told me, I had to then walk a number of city blocks on foot to find her apartment. She was waiting outside so she could guide me through the maze once inside the complex.

Of course, I gave her a long drawn out kiss and held her tight against my body. I fit in all her curves and felt all the soft places. It hadn't held a woman in a number of years notwithstanding the times that Julie had come to visit while I had been in the prison and that had been quite limited.

I was nervous as a church mouse. Now I had expected: pipe cleaning, a romp in the hay, intercourse -for God's sake. It had been so long since it wasn't my imagination that had to be enough. Now here I was here with Julie, for she was my girl, right? We had done the time together and last I understood we had been engaged to be married. I took that for granted since we hadn't been able to have the ceremony, because I had been away, not of my own free will.

The suspense was mounting and I was becoming more and more excited as the seconds passed. As I was planning in my mind, my breath quickened. About to make my move, a feeling, you could say, moved over me and I just knew. Julie drew guns blazing, "Matt, I have been seeing someone else." It was like swallowing down the wrong tube. It seemed like I couldn't breathe all of a sudden. All that came out my mouth searching for words to say was: "How long?" The question didn't really seem to matter, though it fumbled out of my mouth.

"About two months," she replied. This had been exactly what I had been feeling for the last few months. I couldn't fathom how she had stayed with me for so many years and then to just write me off so close to what I thought the finish line.

Our next moments were odd. I felt the world had just spun me around quite violently. Julie broke the ice and said, "You are not going to change, Matt." She softened the blow by handing me an activated cell phone. It seemed to me to be a way to reach out without reaching out. After giving me a broken heart, Julie handed me a wall hanging which was a picture that had once hung on the wall of our last apartment.

Art was the one thing Julie had left me with when it came down to what I had taken from that relationship of many years. Betrayed after my last years were consumed with the dreams of a life with one whom I truly loved; it was as if it were ripped like a carpet from under me. I left shortly after without even a kiss, or at least I was reeling too heavy to remember my departure.

I returned from a long bus ride back to the inner city, to a house, among prosperous drug houses to lick my wounds.

During the next couple of days, I was able to meet up with the parents of my youth whom had done their best in raising me. Knowing that I was starting over from nothing, they took me shopping for clothes, took me out to dinner and gave me all my dad's clothes that he had from storage that he never wore. This time with loved ones had been so much needed. The food was a welcomed en devour, for the restaurant is a far cry in comparison to the processed food of an institution that I had grown so accustomed to. I accepted this all, gratefully. A final gift was a crisp one hundred dollar bill as they dropped me off at the bus stop once again. In their elderly, retired ages, they no longer felt comfortable driving through the inner city.

Chapter 27

"Love, friendship, respect do not unite people As much as a common hatred for something."

--Anton Chekhov

Through the next week, for whatever reason, Julie called me often. I am still not sure if it was due to her having second guesses on her decision, but, nevertheless, talking with her certainly didn't make my position any easier.

The idea of a halfway house, in a transitional living center is to allow you the time to accustom yourself back into society. With this time, you are to find a job and hopefully become a productive member of society preparing for living on your own. In my past, I had worked with a friend doing demolition for a construction company. I had also helped in routine maintenance in rental properties painting, simple electrical wiring, roofing and tuck-pointing a brick building. But for the record, my work history was quite sporadic. The thought of factory work to me was deplorable. Someone once told me, "Find something you love doing and get paid for it." For myself, I found that to be quite elusive.

As time slipped away, so was every bit of the hope and dreams I had while incarcerated. If you're a stranger to incarceration, when one is incarcerated, with the ability to be released at some point in the relative future, being different than one who has no projected release date, one plans and organizes their thoughts, building velocity as like a penny dropped from the Sears Tower in Chicago. Just as when that penny stops, it is at the end of a journey. The criminal has planned for this time years and years, moment by moment. You have only made it through by looking to the short term: canteen, recreation, meals, school and the last count time of the day. We plan for: release, sex, food; and we get loose usually with intoxicants. But then therein lays the problem for myself. There is now nothing much to look forward to. The reality, that all has changed while you were away, is a huge punch in the gut. This is where it all comes crashing down. For so many the look for the heavy artillery, the heavy drugs with the big reward of bliss seems the best option if you discount the past.

My brother knew what I was going through for he himself had had his time spent and released from jails and prisons. I think he realized everything I had planned had been planned to be done together with Julie. I talked to him often on the phone trying to keep thoughts from the constant flurry of the drug houses next door.

I was bored out of my mind. My mind seemed to be working overtime when the cell phone pulled me from my obsessing. I answered it with, "Hey". It could only be Julie, my parents, or my brother Randy calling, so I skipped the formalities. It was my brother's voice on the other line. He said, "Pack your shit. I have a surprise and I am outside." I had given him the address prior hoping my brother would send me some cash, because cash is always good. I hung up the phone.

In trotted down the stairs and parked on the street was my big, brother Randy and my son Matthew, whom had grown a bunch since seeing him last a couple of years ago. They were leaning up against the car like some hooligans. My brother was puffing on a cigarette that never seemed to leave his hand, and Matthew was high with anxiety, like a puppy that bubbled with excitement and couldn't sit still. My son had grown. He had shot up like a turnip; early teens, he was gaining a bit of weight and muscle too.

Of course, I hugged them both. I got smart and asked, "So did you come all this way, driving three and a half hours to bring me some money?" Randy didn't bat an eye, but instead asked, "Where's your shit?" This is when the other convict that I shared the apartment with came barreling down the stairs and into the street. I introduced my family, for what reason, I don't know, other than just trying to be polite, for I surely didn't see myself coming back to this god forsaken city any time soon. I was leaving this slum for a small town, right off of the Mississippi river. I was headed once again to the country, to the river where the eagles fly.

Leaving the city , I called my parole agent to no avail, but decided to leave her the message that I was moving out of the city and county. I left her my next address, where I would be staying, on that old town road.

My son Matthew wasn't able to go to the country with Randy and I, for he still had school to attend. Before dropping him off at his mother's, we went out for dinner and hung out which I hadn't been able to do in the last two years. It was damn good to see my son. In that moment it all became clear for just a moment. I finally comprehended that friends do come and go and are never to be considered in it for the long haul. As you make your journey thru time, I learned, family is the only thing that is important for they are with you through all the struggles. Love doesn't dissolve because you are far away or doing time or because you live your life differently than they live theirs. Love overcomes all. Things you wouldn't accept as behaviors from others, family forgives and accepts regardless.

I do say, what I had portrayed to my son as the "normal family" was far from the one I had known growing up.

Chapter 28

"The whole law of human existence consists in nothing other than a man's always being able to bow before the immeasurably great."

--Fyodor Dostoyevsky

Being in the county, living in a trailer the only place other than the bar to hang out is on the internet. I grew quite accustomed to chat rooms. I reconnected with old buddies from grade school, for God's sake. I thought this was pretty awesome; though, I had only been gone and out of the loop for two years.

Randy, my brother, worked in a factory in a supervisor's position. Things seemed to have changed so drastically, but yet not so much. Randy had always been a hard worker, and had been paid well for it. The way I saw it, he had given up his own dream to make someone else's a reality.

I hung out on the internet. Dating websites became as big a routine as morning coffee. I was glued to the laptop and visited many websites that it was quite normal to interact in the nude. Sex acts themselves were quite enticing. Coming fresh out of prison and no girlfriend or partner, I became addicted almost immediately.

When Randy was home he was on the internet also. He had met a much younger woman than himself on a popular website. Her name was Missy, and Missy had two young children. She was pregnant with the third. I kinda think Randy was thinking, "the ready-made family".

He started to spend nights at Missy's, for her apartment was much closer to Randy's work. At least, this was the excuse he was trying to sell. Soon she she gave birth to another little girl. This made two girls and one spoiled little boy.

The trailer was at times lonely, but I had the internet and Randy had also put me on his phone plan. When the stillness and quiet would get to great, I would go to the bar for a drink or two, maybe three.

It being the dead of winter and this being a trailer home that had no insulation, it was common for me to wake with frozen pipes. This meant no running water until Randy got his ass home, and after borrowing a friends kerosene heater. After a very slow process of heating the belly of the trailer, we were able to thaw the pipes. Any time the temperature would drop to single digits, I would have to crank up that heater. While the place smelled of kerosene, I was at least able to keep the water running, in particular the toilet. I found it was particularly hard to make coffee without water flowing in some part of the house, let alone the kitchen.

Alone I faced one thing after another, and I got the idea why Randy wanted someone around. Next the water heater quit running. Randy spent the weekend replacing the water heater with a new one. I kidded him with the comment, "I am going to start breaking things to be sure you are around more often." He wasn't too keen on that idea.

The internet was a source of the big social media sites. I found so many chat sites. One in particular grabbed my attention quick, for you were able to video chat nude. I fell for it, hook, line and sinker. Alone was not looking to be such a bad thing after all.

I soon found an old school mate, that I had lost touch with for many years. I found her on another social media site. Her name was Brandy, and Brandy just so happened to be in the middle of a divorce. We chatted thru text and soon she felt comfortable enough to give me her phone number. As a youth, many years before, I had always had a crush on Brandy, but I had a crush on all the girls at that tender age. But she was a rebel and that was right up my alley. As the dominoes began to fall so did the wall that she had built around her to protect herself. The day came that she told me she wanted to drive the three hours to come and visit.

By now, I rarely ever saw Randy. That little Missy had taken his heart.

Brandy made the three hour trip, and I had to have her call when she was close. The biggest worry was calls dropped; for cell phone coverage was hard to find in that rural part of the state. After once being pulled over by a sheriff, given directions, she found her way thru the trailer park.

When she arrived, I directed her to park the van next to the trailer rather than park in the driveway, in event Randy made it home to the trailer this particular weekend. I liked to keep Randy in the belief he ran things there, for it was his trailer thus ultimately, his maintenance done with his hard earned money.

When Brandy exited her van, I was in a mess of emotion: first- connecting back to the adolescent years of my life, in which Brandy had been a part of that mess. Second-having not had been with a woman in many years, compounding the dilemma by being alone taking stock in live internet porn. I decided, without a second thought, to assault Brandy with kisses, of a desperate nature, as soon as she got out of her, homely, soccer mom's van.

She was a little shocked. I can only figure, it came as quite the surprise. I believe she may have said something to the ring of, "hold up!" I released her and opened the side door of the van and without missing a beat, grabbing her over packed night bag, which I only imagined was part of her overall decision to spend the weekend. I breathed, "Well, come on in if you're coming," as I maneuvered my way past her to the door of the trailer, drunk on desire.

Don't be fooled, for Brandy had the same on her mind, only she held her cards a little closer to the chest than I.

That weekend I cooked for her and we spent most of the time catching up on the years spent from adolescence til the now. Yes, we did find comfort in each other's arms an awful lot that weekend. It was much needed "fun".

In between tumbles in the back bedroom, I noticed Brandy was taking prescription medication regularly, and with a curious and trained eye, I noticed it to have "Morphine sulfate" on the label. Brandy went on to tell me she suffered from some condition, which pronunciation eludes me. Hell or high water, to me, my diet was about to change. I asked her what she all took for pain, and before long, Vicodin and morphine were on the menu. Of course, drunk on sexual desire, I could have asked Brandy for the moon and she would have tried to rein it in.

Some people don't understand why some use drugs. I can put it to you this way, as a better way to understand. It is more like the answer to "Why?" I mean, who doesn't like to wrap a warm blanket around your body on a cold winter night? Who doesn't appreciate air-conditioning on a hot summer day? Both these are answered in a word, "comfort". Opiates bring over-whelming comfort to the body.

Brandy began to visit regularly through the next couple of months; but I also could be found frequently on the internet adult chat rooms. At times I was on the computer while Brandy was there visiting. It never turned out to be an issue, for Brandy occupied herself, when we weren't in the bedroom, on her own interests. Sometimes we just did our own things.

Being cold winters, frozen pipes became a continual problem. My brother's friend Chris always offered a hand with a torpedo heater. He watched how I was managing most often by myself at the trailer. One day, he offered me a job working with him laying conduit for the installation of electricity for new construction or remodel. I had worked in my early years in the work task force maintaining rental properties, so I knew my way around an electrical box. The work became part time. One building in particular was the job which took my time. It was a burned out historical site. It wasn't long before I was rewiring circuit boxes, quite often on morphine.

Life seemed, "with promise".

Brandy continued to make the trip across the state to visit. Sometimes she even brought one or all three of her sons.

Chapter 29

"Since everything in nature answers to a moral power, if any phenomenon remains brute and dark, it is that the corresponding faculty in the observer is not yet active."

--Ralph Waldo Emerson

It wasn't long before my brother Randy brought home, or back to his trailer, his much younger girlfriend and her adolescent, boy, girl, and the newborn. So now there was myself, Randy, his girlfriend Missy, and three children. Let's not forget the dogs, Zeus and Charlie. Zeus being the pit bull, and Charlie the cocker-doodle. So now you can imagine the eight bodies in the trailer, and that isn't counting when Brandy would make the trip about every other week.

Randy and Missy decided to make a home of the trailer. The weekend of the move, it had snowed consistently. Missy's old apartment was, of course, at the bottom of a large bluff. The only access was down a steep, curvy road. I had volunteered, being the dear brother I was, to help in the move. Randy drove a car full of children and Misty in front of me in a four by four pick-up truck. Due to the weather, Randy was driving down the bluff's windy road sideways. He had to ride the brakes. What scared me most was the truck, though a four by four and all-wheel drive, it still was quite hard to maneuver without sliding down the bluff. My biggest worry was that I would somehow rear end my brother and push the carload of kids and adults off the bluff. That day I surely cussed Randy for having to move "on that weekend".

At the gas station across the street, a pair of snowmobiles fueled up for their joy ride, as I set in for the trek back up the bluff loaded with a truck of clothes and toys risking my life on a snowy afternoon, during a snow emergency out in some backwoods town, all for my brother.

We pulled off the move without a hitch, although I don't remember ever being so scared to drive as I had, in my entire life.

After the move, the settling in the trailer was next on the list of "to-dos". Yes, it was a full house and I soon became quite aware of the difference in the behavior of the dogs. Zeus and Charlie were far from used to the chaos that comes along with small children. The running down the halls, the headlocks and pulling of the tails was only the beginning and those animals' nerves were stretched pretty thin. The day came that Charlie that cocker-spaniel and poodle mix snipped and bit the little boy in the face. Not risking infection, Randy took the little guy to the doctor. Next, Charlie was in quarantine with his first of two strikes that could cost him a trip to the pound, to catch the big sleep. Zeus, a seventy pound pit-bull wasn't far behind when I caught him a moment before had a tasty treat of that little boys hindquarters, for that run down the hall was so much fun. Thank my lucky stars that Zeus never made a chew toy of that little boy.

Now hiding in a room watching adult entertainment on the internet or waiting for the shoe to drop between these dogs and children, I was real thankful when Randy's buddy Chris called and offered me a little electrical work to do for some spare coin. It was after working with Chris that he asked me if I would like to work sporadically, at his vineyard. He was trying to have graded Organic. I would do the simple job. It would entail trimming between the grape vines, mowing the field between each row, and cut the alpha-alpha fields with the tracker. I would learn the basics to what it took to have land labeled Organic.

I purchased a thirty-seven foot trailer/camper. Chris laid out the wire from the barn for my electricity. The water for showers and basic needs came from a five hundred gallon tank, which I filled from a freshly drilled well. I set railroad ties in a square box style, and with the help of the tracker, I lifted that tank of water off the ground by six feet. It fed into my trailer. My needs were met after hooking up the propane to fuel the stove and refrigerator.

Next, Chris then purchased the forms and concrete to lay a slab in the barn. We constructed a tidy, little room, complete with electricity and a compost toilet. This was so I didn't have to move the trailer to empty the waste, for I couldn't run the sewage, waste hose onto the land, for it would affect the Organic certification.

Chris utilized my time, by having me disperse mushrooms or fungus, thus cutting down on the labor of line trimming between the vines by occupying the space normally that weeds would have grown between the vines, but now fungus grew in its place. This was more likely the result of over time, I was killing some of the grape vines when while trimming between the hundreds of vines, I would accidentally cut a few at ground level. You can see how this can be counterproductive.

So hey, now I am learning how to grow fungus. It wasn't long before I got the bright idea to grow what are called "magic mushrooms". The mushrooms are known for their hallucinogenic properties for the psilocybin is a type of poison naturally made by the mushroom to ward off animals from eating the fungus. The mushroom has also been known to treat people with depression. I was all for giving it a try. I purchased the spores online from a company in California. I also bought a kit that would teach me how to grow them. With much trial and error, I finally yielded what I thought to be a good amount. By this time, I was just proud that I managed to grow "something" successfully. I probably should have tried to grow tomatoes.

I was now living on the vineyard. Brandy would visit me often, and we would spend most of the summer nights sitting back in fold-up lawn chairs around a campfire after a grill-out of steak and "mushrooms". After a few cock-tails and a couple grams I fed Brandy of my mushrooms, she was giggling like a schoolgirl. It was certainly a night to remember, for between the liquor and a primal need, I had Brandy in the throes of passion crying for just one more time. Not quite sure where some of them bruises came from, but when the sun rose the next morning she was smiling so I twisted her this way and that. I"m still not sure if she was crying or just overcome with the thrills. It must have been alright cause if I remember right, she never told me, "No", even when I flipped and got quite rough with her.

One weekend, I decided to get back to see my brother at his trailer. I knew how Randy liked to spend his weekend, for it was his routine to consume strong drinks and lounge around the eternal campfire he kept alive in an old Weber grill. Yes, you could say, Randy was backwoods country. Invading on his little parade, I brought some fresh picked mushrooms to liven up his personal party. Of course, when I pulled out the baggy of fresh mushrooms from my pocket and offered them to Randy, I saw the smile of his grow from ear to ear. Magic mushrooms are a great party favor. When ingested, they seem to have anyone under the influence of them laugh, and just have a good time. When I handed the bag to Randy, he ate about two grams which was more than adequate. He was in for a real good time. Brandy and I gobbled up the rest in the bag and were off to get groceries from the store before they kicked in on full effect.

We returned with steaks and beer in hand, and after exiting the car and finding Randy in the kitchen, I asked Randy,"How do you feel?" He looked at me with big eyes and a smile on his face. He says, "What did you do to me?" I pulled beers out of the case and distributed to the smiling faces. I don't think Missy knew, for she was occupied with her children. Well, we tapped the bottles cheers and I made the toast, "to brothers and best friends!" I noticed that Randy needed just this to unwind, for he gave me a shit eating grin and stood up to give me a great big bear hug.

We ate and drank beer around his makeshift campsite. I would imagine to the untrained eye, we were just some adults having a good time. Smiles, bonding and many laughs confirmed a moment to be remembered.

It wasn't until much later after the effects of the mushrooms had expired that, while still feeling alright from the alcohol, Randy informed me that I was to be the best man in his wedding. He had asked Missy to marry him. He would adopt the three children, for the biological fathers were all absentee. In all honesty, I was skeptical, for it looked like a lot to handle but I naturally kept it to myself. Missy and the children seemed to be something Randy enjoyed, and I wouldn't place rain on his parade. Maybe, I should have put it into the words he would have understood. To me, it seemed like he was filling the shoes of "Captain save a hoe". Was it up to me to say something that might smash his dreams? I think that it is common sense that told me he was so head over heels, because she was twenty years his junior.

Randy soon started making wedding plans: ordering the lavish invitations, booking the tavern for a large reception, picking the church for the ceremony, tuxedo fittings, and ordering the vast amount of catered food.

Myself, I was going to make this day one to remember. I began to make my own plans over the months. The reception was going to be paramount. I began to put together a large assortment of aerial display fireworks. Electronic ignition system and the biggest and loudest display that i could put together.

With everything that was going on, Brandy had made some of her own decisions. She informed me that she had decided to start looking for a place and wanted to move to the area. She tried to tell me that this decision she had made wasn't just because of her desire to be around me. She went on to tell me that she thought the area was so beautiful, she wanted to have her kids enjoy the country living. I like to think it was because of me that she wanted to move. After looking at several trailer homes in the area, Brandy found one that was less than five miles from the vineyard I was situated on.

Of course, with Brandy planning for the move by packing herself and three teenage boys, it was left to me to begin the overhaul of painting the inside of her newly purchased trailer. One final trip before the move, she and the boys came to finished up with the remained of the painting. The next week, Brandy and her boys made the move to the country.

One day, Randy called me. I immediately knew by the sound of his voice that something was certainly askew. Something was seriously wrong. Being brothers, as well as best friends, I was the one Randy laid his burdens on and I was happy for it. Randy went on to inform me, that he had come home early from work, and found Missy "with company". He went on to tell me that although the date of marriage was set, there was trouble in paradise. He informed me of the gritty details: sexual relations diminished, and continuous, frivolous arguments over nothing. Trouble had been brewing for weeks. Surprising her, by coming home from work early and finding her with some random dude in the house brought the acknowledgement that he hadn't known how many others had been there. Then he dropped the bomb. Missy and the children had just moved out.

Devastated, he was. What is one to say to another that had been betrayed by love? I stayed on the phone, jumped in the car, and before long was at his trailer. We walked to one of the two bars that were in the town, and we drank to sorrow. The death of two women in Randy's life, and now the loss of his fiance, all of whom he loved, his life seemed to be crumbling to pieces.

I stayed the night and a couple of nights after that. Randy and I just hung out when he was working obsessively for most of the hours of the day. I guess being the supervisor at his job, which he seemed proud of, had its perks.

One night, Randy called me while I was lounging at my own trailer. He told me to get my ass over to his house; he had come across some "party favors". This is the true beginning of the nightmare.

Chapter 30

"I will show you fear in a handful of dust"

--T.S. Elliot

The thing about being an drug addict that uses the drug by way of a syringe is that when not using a bio-hazard syringe collection box, which are readily available for free in most major cities through a program designed to prevent the spread of disease, an addict will tend to hide a syringe out of sight, but yet readily available and closely accessible. In Randy's trailer, there was quite a number stashed over the many years of living there from time to time.

When I arrived at Randy's trailer, I found him quite excitable. To all appearances, physically, he was no longer suffering, by basking in depression; but by the looks of the trailer, there had been many weeks of neglect in keeping up the place. He pulled a three by six inch zip lock baggie from his pocket. In it were what appeared to be small crystals resembling rock salt but just a bit finer.

There was a type of what appeared to be joy dancing in Randy's eyes.

I followed him as he made his way through the hall, dodging Charlie and Zeus who seemed awfully glad to see me. In the bathroom, I located one of my old syringes from under the vanity. I cleaned it out by filling a number of times with water to be sure I wouldn't get sick by injecting some virus or bacteria.

The process was easy. Randy showed me that you take the plunger out of the syringe. He then took a couple of these crystals from the bag and inserted them where the plunger had been recessed. Inserting the plunger, following the crystals, then Randy used the syringe to draw up water. He shook the syringe and the crystals dissolved in the water of the syringe.

The injection, into the veins, of your arm, fills your mouth with a medicine taste much like when being given a shot in an IV port before going into a medical practiced surgery. The rush that over takes your body is comparable to the drop from a mighty, high roller coaster, and sustaining this rush for a period of many hours, if not several days. With an energy that lasts for days, matched with an ambition that supports an accomplishment of any project, the stimulation is more addicting than any drug I had ever used before. Very different from the use of the drug cocaine, there was no need for more than a small amount.

With prior drug habits, the belief of "more is better "attitude can easily spin you into the unneeded use of more, which can lead you into vivid hallucinations brought on by the drug. This use of the drug, lasting for several days, without sleep or a desire to eat or drink mental deterioration will soon follow and is to be expected.

At this point, Randy decided that he was going to go back to the city, a forty-five minute drive one way, to purchase more of the drug-methamphetamine.

I had decided to stay at the trailer while he went about his own mission of accumulating the drug. I went about cleaning Randy's trailer from top to bottom and from one end to the other. Washing dishes, vacuuming, scouring tables, as well as dusting seemed to be a great idea in helping pull my brother from the chasm of depression he had been wallowing in.

I waited for what later was determined to have been almost twenty four hours before abandoning the thoughts of more along with Randy's return. I scurried off back towards the vineyard. On the way, I decided to drive by Brandy's trailer. How many actual sunrises had passed I had no clue, but I was feeling the guilt as if I had done something wrong. This feeling was compounded, because I had never not seen Brandy since she and her boys had moved up to the country.

When I got to her trailer, I decided to drop in. I can only imagine that it was obvious of my border line psychotic state. I had been picking at my face like a teenager with acne. I had always had the habit of nervous picking at myself, but this time it was severely compounded. I had meticulously pulled out all the hairs along my bottom lip. This would have appeared to any other as a type of burn all along the extent of the skin below my lip. My mental health was in peril. I was schizophrenic, hearing and seeing things in the worst way.

When Brandy awakened by me , one look and she got up and gave me one of her morphine pills to dull the pain, from the damage, I had inflicted to my face. This also helped to calm me down. Exhausted as my body was; it was about an hour and I was fast asleep.

Picture painted, I knew that the use of methamphetamine was dangerous. I wanted piles of it. Having lived with my own depression my whole life, a drug that allowed me to function was too good to be real. I had totally neglected to heed the taste, of the aftereffects, of delirium. The price to pay, would be my soul.

After a couple of days, of recuperation, as in sleep, hydration, as well as, back to taking my prescribed medication, which was much needed for stabilizing my mental health when not on the drug, life seemed to snap back into routine.

Daily conversations with Randy were a regular. He informed me he had been in touch with our mutual friend of old, Shelly. He had found her thru social media. We had a good laugh, when I informed him, that I also had been in communication with her recently.

Randy called one day and informed me he had won two tickets in a raffle at work. The tickets were to a Green Bay Packers football game. As the date came closer, he seemed to be bursting with excitement. The plan was that he was to drive and swing by to pick up his daughter, Meghan. He planned to enjoy the game and excitement as well as a bonding moment with his darling daughter.

Well when the big day of the game came, Meghan called me.

She asked, "Have you heard from my dad?"

Now this was an odd question, knowing what the plan that had been established for this particular day. I told dear little Meghan, I would find him, since I hadn't heard from him either. I called repeatedly to his cell phone, and it went to voicemail immediately. To me, this indicated, the phone was shut off. I thought something was definitely, "Off".

I had no other choice but to drive the thirty miles to his trailer to check on him. Brandy drove with me, and as we pulled onto the street which his trailer was located on, I noticed legs protruding from under the pick-up truck that had been at his trailer from when he had brought me back up north. This is the same pick-up truck that Randy had told me his plan had been to salvage the truck, for it would cost too much money to get it running once again.

Randy's own car was not in the driveway either.

The whole situation was just strange.

It was Randy that crawled out from under that pick up truck, and it was obvious, something was terribly wrong. He stood up, and as I got out the car to investigate the situation, he looks at me and says,"They put a tracker on my truck!"

That truck hadn't run for quite a long while.

I asked Randy, "Where is your phone?"

"I lost the charger, and it is dead!" He replied.

Often, in the past, when Randy would use the drug cocaine, he would clench his jaw, or he would roll his jaw unaware. This same action was in full affect. I knew he was drugged to capacity by the telltale signs.

It took me quite a spell to finally draw out from him the events, or his perception of the whole night past. It started with purchasing methamphetamine after work. Randy went on to tell me, after stopping on the side of the road, he had injected some of the meth that he had purchased on the way home. He went on to explain that he had then been pulled over by a county sheriff. Well as I gathered through the course of his interpretation, he hadn't actually been pulled over, but he had, being under the influence of the drug, become extremely paranoid and had pulled into the rest area on the side of the road. He had been sitting in his car when a county sheriff also pulled into the lot. At this point, Randy informed me, he had, in attempt to avoid a possible arrest, put the zip lock baggie of meth into his mouth and swallowed it.

The sheriff was stopping to see if he had needed some sort of help, but after assessing the behavior of my brother, he suggested that Randy call for a ride or walk home the remainder of the way to his house. I believe the officer may have believed that Randy was having a severe mental health crisis, but would accept no health. The officer left him there at the rest stop, but Randy said he thought the officer had put some sort of electronic tracking system in the wheel well of his car. This is where Randy probably lost his phone charger.

He had ate over a gram of meth. This was enough to keep him spun and awake, most likely in extreme psychosis for the duration of three days. He had walked back home from the rest stop. There was no tracking system on the car, but he thought maybe he should check the rundown, salvage pick up at his trailer just in case a tracking device had by some chance been installed on that vehicle. He was a mess.

Obviously, Randy was in no condition to go to the football game with his daughter. They would have missed quite a bit of it even had the time it took in transport would not have been the issue, let alone his delirium.

I had Randy call Meghan on my phone as Brandy, Randy, and I headed down the road to the nearest store, thirty miles away, to purchase another charger for my spun out brother. Of course, after talking with her dad, Meghan told me that I needed to take her dad to the mental hospital to be evaluated.

Purchasing the charger for the phone and getting us back to Randy's trailer proved to be difficult, for meth is known for its persistent distractions which Randy was drowning in. The store was the biggest fun park, although having to stop at every gas station for this or that on Randy's whim proved cumbersome.

After returning to Randy's trailer and babysitting for a number of hours, Randy drifted off to sleep with the help of a couple of sleeping pills. Brandy and I breathed a breath of relief as we now knew him to be safe for the time being. We locked the door on our way out and made our way back towards the vineyard for some private time.

Chapter 31

"Brothers and sisters are closer than hands and feet"

--A Byzantine Proverb

Brandy and I bounced between her trailer and mine. There were nights we slept apart. Being in our early forties us both had our own routines.

One particular day, I had been up early and was well caffeinated, and I believed I was up on my own with free run on a morning at Brandy and family's trailer. Well I ducked out of the bedroom to facilitate a brew of more coffee and came into the living room to find Brandy's youngest boy at the ripe age of twelve, masturbating in the wide open while lying on the couch watching a cartoon on the television. Now, I had known for him to be awake fiddling around on the computer before school, but this was something different. This act of self-appreciation to cartoons was the last thing that I had expected this morning, or frankly, at any point, noon or evening, ever. Now the kid was going to town on himself and I was past the point of being noticed as I scurried through the living room. What was I supposed to do? What would you do? I barreled through to brew that pot of Jo. Of course, I was trying my best not to fall over, or even have my laughter heard. I didn't want to scar the boy psych, for God's sake. On my return through the room I held my gaze down and to limit the embarrassment of the boy, I pretended that I saw nothing and none the wiser to this explosive issue.

I should have kept this jewel of knowledge to myself, but I didn't. I brought the humor to Brandy's attention as she saturated her system with freshly brewed coffee, a was our morning routine catching her the moment she opened her eyes. She found the finding a bit more humorous than I. I felt bad for the kid, because this is normal behavior for adolescent boys of his age. And whatever young man says different, I do believe him to be lying.

Brandy made this a family joke and told her older two sons of my findings. That kid will probably never live it down, but I'm sure if the need arises; he will find a much more personal place to have his way.

As the summer past, September brought cool winds. With cooler weather, there was less to do at the vineyard. It had always been just a place that I could have on my own, a place to spend quiet time by myself.

There was never a certain schedule to keep while on the vineyard, and this had been great in light of the fact that my mental health had always been a bit of a hindrance in what is considered "stable" in society. A "normal" job often requires consecutive days of labor. Managing myself allowed for the space that I needed. I think that Chris and his wife Ann, the vineyard owners, great friends of mine and my brother, used the whole vineyard experience: owning my own place, working at my own pace, and a small allowance; to build my self-esteem. However, I did pay them back tenfold when it came time to throw bales of hay that he planted for harvest which included the manual labor, of filling the barn for storage of the hay, for the animals they owned.

The vineyard, being my responsibility was also my place of enjoyment. Randy often stopped by, sometimes without notice which was a pleasant surprise. We harvested mushrooms that I had sown to combat the weeds between the vines on the now "organic" vineyard. We grilled steaks and drank cold beer as we watched Charlie and Zeus, Randy's dogs; take full advantage of the wide open space to run about. Charlie was in constant chase of the butterflies, and Zeus, the pit bull chased Charlie.

I have realized that as we bustle through this life, always seeming too busy, we neglect to recall or even remember to enjoy the moment at hand. Always thinking of the future, we miss enjoying the content moment we in which we are fluid.

My Brother Randy's calls to me began to taper off over the next couple of weeks. I came to the conclusion that he was most likely internet trolling for women in the area.

Brandy and I were to meet Randy for drinks at a tavern that had live music scheduled not far from the vineyard. Randy finally showed up quite a bit later than the plan that we had to meet. When I asked him what took him so long, Randy went on to inform us he had been with a woman he had met internet surfing on a dating website. To me this was a good sign of things returning to the normal. As long as he was dating, it was a good sign. The way I saw it was that if he was dating, he was less likely to be basking in deep depression over the break up with Missy.

There came the day that Brandy and I decide to stop down on a surprise visit to check on him. I found out what the true reason for Randy's recent lack of communication. That old friend known from adolescent age and old mischievous girlfriend of Randy's Shelly had moved across the state and now was living once again with Randy.

Seeing Shelly was nice, for who doesn't like to see and visit age old friends of their past. The key word in this is to "visit". As long as I had known Shelly, I knew her to be trouble. What I mean by trouble would be, a real unpredictable woman, who for no other reason, always seemed to have an ax to grind. If that wasn't enough of an explanation, you sure don't turn your back towards her for she would most likely stick a knife in your back. Unpredictable is the best way to explain her. I also knew her to have serious addiction issues, and as of late I knew that before she found her way to Randy's, her husband had been filling her with meth amphetamines.

I knew that it wouldn't be long before the roommate relationship, he wanted me to believe that was taking place, would be the cement shoes, or collision that this was going to none other than be, besides the meth that was bound to be the noose to kill.

All my years of being the little brother to Randy, it was known to me that he had a paranoia regarding the fidelity of the woman he surrounded and accompanied him, including Shelly. And it sure wasn't unheard of for him to accuse me of wrangling his women. That was not my style, but I wouldn't be surprised if this was due to him wrestling his own demons. It seemed that even with Brandy sitting next to me I caught that look in his eye that he had issue with the belief Shelly was communicating with me. Realizing the thought was probably fueled by meth use, for I could read it in his demeanor. I think to give you an idea of the severity of this delusion, I can explain it like this: if I were to be behind the kitchen bar getting a cup of coffee, and Shelly was in the kitchen with me, Randy would believe in his own mind that Shelly and I had our pants off and were somehow sexually active unnoticed to others. This is no exaggeration. The drug has a way of convincing you to believe whatever your fears are, they are surely taking place.

Brandy and I left after a while for the tension was high before leaving the trailer. My competent, sober, responsible, and passionate brother began to slip away before my eyes.

It was soon after this that the cool of October set in. Brandy spent less nights at my small summer trailer and I spent more nights at her trailer. Spending time with Brandy was nice, but as in any relationship, compromise is forever an ensuing matter.

I was a cigarette smoker and she was not. I am told that, to a non-smoker, tobacco and nicotine leaves a foul smell blanketed on everything. This became the daily gripe from Brandy and her kids, and truth be told, I wasn't always on the ball with ashing my ashes into the ashtray. My ashes often found their way to the ground, more specific: the carpet, and tables, missing the ashtray. Well before long, I found myself like Dino from the Flintstones cartoon, stuck outside in the cold, to measure the pleasure of smoke versus the cold of the coming winter.

One day I received a call from Randy. I could tell by the awkwardness of his voice that something was quite "off" with him. I knew he was probably stoned on meth amphetamines. He asked if I could meet him in a small town situated about on the halfway mark between his trailer and Brandy's. His request was for me to bring him some sort of pill that he could take that might allow him some much needed sleep. He went on to explain that he had been on a binge for several days, he had used up his sick days at work and was hoping to be back in the swing of things or lose his job.

Understanding that his state of mind was clouded most likely from lack of sleep in several days, I tried to have him to understand that I had no pill to fix him. I had anti-depressants but that was no quick fix. I knew he was thinking opiates such as used for pain. I was prescribed opiates for pain, but what I had would need to last me till my doctor's appointment. I had stretched myself thin, for I had a habit of taking more than I was to take often limiting my supply.

I met Randy on our planned meet. I gave him some pills I had for sleep aide, but more or less came to the meet to show him support emotionally. We sat by the car and watched an eagle, whose height must have been four feet tall, as it tore meat from a fresh roadkill. To me this signified the reason we had both left the big city, too have a chance against addiction and to live "where the eagles soar". Randy left me that day and I surely felt the sadness, for drugs were again pulling at his soul.

Chapter 32

"A little poison, now and then, maketh pleasant dreams and much poisons a last for a pleasant death."

--Friedrich Nietzsche

It was three days past when the ringing melody of my phone captured me from my sleep. I had been spending more nights with Brandy at her home. When I answered the phone, it was Shelly's voice I heard frantic on the other end. Her words would seer into my memory for a lifetime. "Can you bring him back if his skin is grey?" she asked. Still groggy and fighting sleep for it was seven o'clock as I looked at the alarm. I asked," What did you say?" "If he is grey, can you still bring him back?" she repeated. This time the gravity of the statement hit me. Only imagining what may be at stake, I breathed fury into the phone and answered, "Call an ambulance, I am on my way!"

Brandy too had been awakened to the call, and hearing the desperation and onslaught of pain that had begun to grip my soul, as the probable outcome was finding every scenario played out from my mind. Brandy was up and dressed, and seeing the shock that was holding me, she said, "Let's go, I will drive."

Randy's trailer was thirty to forty minutes drive on any normal day. When we turned into the trailer park twenty three minutes had elapsed since we left Brandy's home. A couple of trailers before the lot that my brother rented for his trailer, the unbearable shock took hold. As Brandy pulled the van to the side of the road, for she could travel no further by vehicle do to the crime scene tape that was meant to stop any further traffic from that wing of the trailer park; we witnessed two officers and what figured to be the medical examiner taking a black body bag from my brother's residence to a waiting van.

I now knew without doubt that my best friend, my son's uncle, my nieces father, the man I had shared life since my birth, my big brother Randy no longer drew breathe in this world. The loss began to consume me that very moment as if a forest fire burning out of control.

Charlie, my brother's cocker doodle, had fled the trailer while the door had been open. Little Charlie followed the men carrying my dead brother. Soon he dashed through the officer's legs. Charlie jumped into the van and guarded his master. I could hear his cry from the van as it escalated to a howl and a sharp bark. Charlie made for a beeline out of the van holding my brother's body straight towards Brandy's vehicle for which he was familiar.

Well Charlie wasn't the only one to notice the van. Within a moment's notice a man began his approach. He wore plain dress clothes and came from a newer model pick-up truck; I recognized to often be used by law enforcement. The man was a detective I had encounters with among prior dates.

The gravity of the situation brought the agony of loss. The pain brought tightness in my chest as tears ran from my eyes down my face. There was no denying the truth.

When the cop made it to the passenger's side window, I rolled it down. His rhetoric was to the point. His demeanor was firm.

"When were you here last, Matt?"

"It's been a while." I stated.

"Do you know his dealer?" The detective investigated

"No", I returned.

"When are you gonna learn drugs are no good, Matt?" With that he walked away.

It was a slap in the face. My older brother is obviously dead and this cop wants to throw cheap shots, was all that went through my mind. How dare he talk without compassion! As a man that has had deep seeded addiction issues, now assumed criminal, it was known to me that you will find no empathy from these professionals, for the have seen too much darkness in their work.

I was now tasked to inform family. My first call was to the people I came to call mother and father, for they gave me the foundation after the trauma of losing my mother at a tender age. They were my father's sister, which made them my aunt and uncle before the adoption. This was a loss to all who had known Randy, but shock of loss made it all about me. I was blank, shattered, and cascading a precipice of abyss. My mother tasked in informing the family and his daughter of the death.

A good man left the world that day, leaving an emptiness that would scar my heart, as well as many who knew him.

Shelly who had been staying with Randy, made a statement to police after her arrest on the scene. She claimed Randy and her had ingested meth amphetamine for the last week. In order to take the edge of Randy had purchased a small amount of heroin on his last trip to the city. I am quite familiar that opiates can and will in smaller amounts can comfort and relieve pain in the body as you experience the withdrawal from heavy drugs. Randy and Shelly had limited consumption of essential nutrition, were dehydrated from loss of water in the body for approximately a week. After finding rest, unfortunately, Randy's body was exhausted to the extreme that the heroin stopped his breathing, leading to respiratory failure. Having been a heroin addict earlier in life and escaping to the country, to change his life, Randy should have known the power of the heavy drug.

After the fact, Shelly later informed me that after a week on meth they injected a small amount of heroin which allowed an appetite. They had then taken a walk with Charlie. Shelly said that Randy must have taken another shot, for after he laid down to rest, she thought him to be snoring quite loudly. What she didn't know, before she got aggravated and went to sleep on the couch, is that this body behavior after use of a heavy sedative is called a death rattle.

Randy had died according to the medical examiner's findings at 4:30 am. Three hours before Shelly's call.

After my brother's death, the stability I had once clung to was no longer there to anchor me. I began to drink heavily. I was severely intoxicated by early afternoon sunk into sweat and slumber.

When Shelly was released from the jail after the investigation of my brother's death, Brandy allowed her to stay with us in Brandy's trailer. Michelle was quick to join me in my drinking. Brandy decided she didn't wish to be involved in this behavior and asked me to leave.

I took my dog Charlie to the vineyard. It was frigged cold. The heater didn't work, although I had bought the parts to fix it. I could never figure the circuitry, so I used the stove and a fan to heat the place with propane. Brandy would allow me to come and shower at her trailer. My trek thirty yards to the barn to use the compose toilet in the snow was brutal in the frigid temperatures.

I was contacted by an insurance company that Randy had obtained through work. The life insurance benefit was seven thousand dollars. Unfortunately, I owed a large bill for past child support payments. They claimed four thousand after I pleaded with child support to allow me to keep some of the cash. Looking for a way to make some cash, when the insurance company asked if I knew the whereabouts of Shelly, I told them I would see what I could do to find her. When I did, I struck the deal to give her the information to claim the monies for a price of one thousand dollars. I never saw a penny of it. Instead Shelly told me God told her to use the money elsewhere. My niece, Meghan was awarded twenty five thousand dollars and paid a large portion of it for her father's funeral.

Chapter 33

"The safest road to hell is the gradual one-the gentle slope, soft underfoot, without turnings, without milestones, without sign posts."

--C.S. Lewis

I got a job at a hardwoods lumber plant, but my addiction was found full throttle when I met guys of the like mind at work.

If things couldn't seem to get any worse, Chris the owner of the vineyard, my summer time employed, called me via telephone to demand that he would like to see me off his land. At the time, I couldn't figure out where this hostility came from, but had no standing to question him. Working twelve hour shifts, it wasn't long before I found a different residence. It was a rooming house, and it was the only place I found that I could have Charlie. It wasn't long until I missed too many days at work and was finally fired.

I had always had a problem in staying stable and maintaining responsibility. I would use pretty much any drug I could find. The death of my older brother only fueled my obsession with heavy drug use. If I thought that I was suffering severe addiction at any other prior time, it was nothing compared to crisis of loss affected me. I often would lie to myself that street drugs didn't have much impact on my mental health, but I soon believed I no longer needed nor would I take the drugs prescribed to me by the psychiatrist. On the appointments I did keep, the doctors would notice my behavior was radical and would ask me to take a drug screen. Of course, I never took the screenings and soon my prescriptions were no longer filled because they themselves were control substances that could be abused.

Depression, drug withdrawal and the continued contemplation of suicide were a cycle I would be in constant battle.

On occasion I would work for cash a day here and a day there in a private kitchen that the owner's delight was to pickle cucumber, can peaches and his specialty, to make sauce for spaghetti. The pay was minimal but having no regular income this came in handy.

With the battery of life struggles, as I often have done in the past, I began to spend what little money I could acquire on the initiate of by brother's resolve, methamphetamine. I really have no understanding of the effects on the brain, but have been told that it rewires, in a sense, the human pathways of the brain.

I can describe to the non-user how the effects of snorting, smoking through the pipe, or injection takes hold of the body. After ingestion there is a burning if snorted any other route is the immediate euphoria of exaltation. There is an immediate burst of energy that doesn't leave you for periods of eight to ten hours. This is use of a small amount, costing around ten dollars. There is no need or overpowering desire to do more. Exhausting exercising physically became easy. The problem therein lies with the effects to one's mental health. Drinking water or other fluids can be easily forgotten, causing dehydration. Remembering to eat also is one of the problem because there is no hunger which can lead to malnutrition. As sleep becomes less of a need, mental health deteriorates and the hallucinations abound.

Then one evening after using meth, I found myself in contemplation of my past relationship of Brandy while cruising around the neighborhoods of the small town. It happened to be the middle of the night and was dark, but in my delusional reality I witnessed her being pulled into a house which appeared violently. I thought maybe she had been walking near the rooming house when attacked, though she lived no less than ten miles away. To me, it had appeared that she had went knocking on a house door and was grabbed, as in abducted, and pulled into the residence by the some violent individual. I got out of the car and crept up to the house and thought what I believed may have been screaming. I thought maybe they were taking her into the basement for the scream seemed at the edge of my ability to hear. Need I remind the power involved with the use of methamphetamine?

I took my phone from my pocket and dialed 911 emergencies.

I said, "A woman has been taken into a home by force. Come quickly!"

I gave 911 the street and address where I was located, and soon a police cruiser stopped near my car that I had sat in anticipating their arrival. I explained what I saw and the immediately went to the front door of the house I led them too to begin pounding on the door. The lights came on and an elderly lady answered the door. I didn't think the investigation should have stopped by talking with the woman, but the officer informed me we had awakened the elderly woman and that no crime or kidnapping had happened to their knowledge at this address.

The officer's attention then became directed at me. I was put through a sobriety test which somehow I passed. The officers then decided top rummage my dead brother's vehicle. Through the search, they discovered a pill bottle of mine containing a heavy tranquilizer prescribed to me. I believe, thinking I may be having a psychotic break or some other mental health issue, they took pity on me. I was instructed to walk home and not to drive my car until I have had some rest.

As I look back, it was no wonder that I was unable to maintain stable employment. I believed that I was doing things much more efficiently, but truth be told, the days had turned into a blur. In my own reality, I believed I had been accomplishing great things in leaps and bounds. The truth of the matter, I was just really high on the drug.

With no heed to the officer's warning, a couple of hours later I was on my way to a job interview. Jobs in the rural areas are quite hard to come by, and often you are left after acquiring the job long travel time, most often more than a half hour commute.

I arrived and was given a tour of the factory but felt as if I was being constantly sized up or taken inventory of mental capacity. I left knowing it was a good chance that I would not hear back from this employer. I tried several times to reestablish contact after I had gotten that much needed rest , but I do believe the damage was done on first impression.

Still living at the rooming house, I happened upon a woman, whom had been a friend of my brother Randy. They had met and I was later introduced while this woman and her daughter stayed on the property my brother had rented to store such equipment as: riding lawn mowers, a bobcat (being a small front end loader), trailers and a dump truck. Through the summer, we also chopped, stacked and stored firewood on that same property. I had met her in the midst of this time. Her name was Pearl and her daughter's name Angel.

After finally acquiring a job, I would find Shelly, my brother's girlfriend at the time of his death, an old childhood friend, and Charlie sitting in the air conditioned and cooled room of Pearl's. Shelly would take Charlie out to do his business while I was at work. She also kept him in exercise by walking him.

Along with a regular job at another lumber yard assembling framing tresses for new construction, the money soon began to trickle back into my life. The rent got paid. My pocket began to fill with cash and working such long hours I had not much time to spend it.

Shelly began to be a regular fixture in my little room. She would disappear for hours with Charlie. One day, going for a walk with the two of them, I found we stopped at an apartment only a half a block away. This the day I would meet a younger woman by the name of Tasha. I soon found by way of conversation that she was ten years younger than I. The apartment was her ex-husbands, with whom Tasha had shared placement of her daughter Trinity. I gathered that Tasha didn't live there, but she would often crash on the living room floor; oddly, with her boyfriend at the time named Steve, and Steve was a long time old friend of her ex-husband named Rob.

Shelly and I left soon after introductions. By the smell of the place I had known they had been smoking marijuana for which I had to decline any ingestion, for the drug is known to store in one's fat cell for up to thirty days and I happened to be under supervision by the department of corrections. Shelly informed me that Tasha would soon have acquired a bottle of morphine pills and was willing to sell some. I had to work so I left Shelly with a hundred dollar bill and instructions to acquire as many as possible. I knew Shelly would do some skimming on the transaction, for it is part of her well known reputation. More often than not it isn't worth the hassle of dealing with her. She was a thief to her core. She stole without a conscious.

The next time, without a hitch in acquiring, I cut Shelly out and went straight to Rob's house. Most often Tasha and her boyfriend were not to be found at Rob's, but I stayed and soon Rob and I became friends.

The day came that I happened by and I was introduced to Tasha's daughter, for Tasha and Steve were there that day among the mess of a living room sleepover. I really didn't know how to act or interact with a ten year old girl. I gave her waist long hair a tug in a playful gesture. Well she got mad and I thought she was gonna cry. Embarrassed and insecure, I apologized. Tasha laughed at me and informed me that her daughter was autistic and the biggest thing, she could not stand her hair to be touched.

It soon became a regular occurrence to meet up with Tasha to buy whatever drug she had access to. Most often it was drug by the name of Suboxone. She radically over charged me, but I didn't much care. She was kind of cute, though it never dawned on me to shoot my shot on any kind of relationship with her.

One day I received a call from Tasha's boyfriend, Steve. The reason he gave was that he needed a place to stay for a couple of weeks until he could find his own apartment. I really didn't know this cat, but I thought I could use some company while I wasn't at work. I let him move in. The way I saw it, it was a favor to Tasha.

As with any residence, the landlord had me have Steve fill out an application for new residence. He filled out the application. I turned it in speedily.

My depression takes hold of my whole existence. Often I cannot even function as a regular member of society. My work performance lacks weight and often missing work becomes the norm. After a spell, knowing my job weighed in the balance, I would make doctors' appointments just to acquire the receipt of visit, for a written excuse for my work absence. Mental health instability along with addictions is a rough life to live. I lost my job again.

Meanwhile my rent is behind and accumulating a negative balance. The management of the rooming house confronts me with a pay or leave notice. When I asked what the eviction was about, he informed me that Tasha and Steve are well known in the community of this small town as severe drug addicts. I was also informed that Steve had lied on his application about his name and past employment. I seemed destined to be homeless with a cocker doodle named Charlie.

I could wager that it had been obvious with signs of my own drug usage and with Steve's appearance on the scene was the tipping point. I came to find out later that Tasha and Pearl were in a dispute over money; which tells me that this was another reason I was put in the spotlight. For doesn't it all comes down to money, at some point?

My days and nights were filled with small trips trying to keep the car warm. My funds of fifty six dollars a week from unemployment dwindled quickly. Charlie and I slept in the packed car, in the parking lot between the rooming house and Rob's apartment.

Chapter 34

"Forgiveness does not change the past; it lays siege to the future."

--Paul Housa

One morning I woke to my cell phone ringing. The call was from Tasha. She informed me she was at the store and wanted to know if I would be willing to pick her up.

Of course, I said, "Sure, why not?"

When I pulled up to the curb in front of the store, she came out of the store, all smiles. I kinda expected her next question. "Do you wanna get high?" With no hesitation I said, "Yes." I had the paraphernalia to accompany the request in a flash.

Tasha pulled out a pill known as hydromorphone. The street name for the drug is pharmaceutical heroine. After the process of breaking down the pill with water, we each injected the liquid that we had divided between the both of us. In sweet bliss I gave a slow look to Tasha noticing the glazed eyes which I am sure matched mine.

Tasha suggested that we stop at her brother's trailer. With an open schedule and nothing to do, I had Tasha direct me to her brother's residence.

Once that we arrived, we went straight inside; for the door was unlocked. Her brother Rick was not home, but his live in girlfriend was in the middle of doing a sink full of dishes. She dried her hands on a towel as Tasha opened the refrigerator and grabbed two sodas and handed me one.

This was right on time for my daily need of sugar and caffeine.

From what I gathered, Tasha's brother Rick was at work.

That is when Tasha threw me a curve ball. She asked Amy, Rick's girlfriend, "Can you give Rick a call and ask if me and a friend can stay here for a while until we find a place to live?" Amy looked at Tasha with a wink and asked, "A friend huh?" Tasha fired back as if I wasn't sitting there, "He's my new boyfriend, and he just doesn't know it yet."

I think in that moment my heart took a good five seconds to beat again.

So here is my life completely broken in pieces. It had been my plan that evening to buy a gallon of gas, soak the car and myself and with the flick of a match, draw an end to my life struggle. Instead this woman, seeming no care in the world, had just basically branded me as her property, her pet project, her boyfriend.

The phone on the counter began to chirp and Amy grabbed and answered it. It was Rick and his answer was "Sure", to us moving our asses into his trailer.

That night Tasha slept with her niece on the floor of the spare bedroom as I slept on the bed pondering had things had transpired so quickly. I soon fell fast asleep. I slept pretty soundly that evening.

The next morning Tasha called her ex-husband and told him to ask Steve to leave and that she wouldn't need to stay there any longer. I was in complete awe, for you really can't make this kind of stuff up.

To make matters more interesting, when I had coffee with Rick, he handed me a hundred dollar bill and mentioned that he had noticed that my registration on the car was overdue.

He says, "That is not a loan. It is a gift to help you get your life in order."

Of course, I'm blown away by his generosity. First letting a stranger move in, and then giving me money for my registration, I was completely baffled.

Tasha and I drove to the department motor vehicles, and with the renewal card I registered the vehicle for another year in my deceased brother's name, for it was still registered in his name.

Next, I had a psychiatrist appointment in which he prescribed me amphetamines for attention deficit disorder. For the next week Tasha and I ingested the whole script in one way or another within the next week. My whole bottle of much needed medication was now empty and it was to have lasted a month.

Now Rick's girlfriend Amy was witness to our behavior which included little sleep and often all night sessions of intercourse. I found amphetamines to to a real way to spice up sex but sleep was lacking. Our actions not only kept us awake but also affected Rick and Amy's sleep.

The relationship between Tasha and me seemed great, but in my past experiences I knew drugs were one way to ruin a good thing. The years of my life had given me an attitude and perception regarding relationships. In my mind I figured my best defense was to have no expectations. When I relayed this idea to Tasha, she just winked at me and with a crooked smile interjected, "Web will just have to see." Her next proclamation was: "Don't worry; we have our whole lives to figure it out." Like a lasso to my heart, expectations grew like an aggressive vine.

Our reckless behavior was also affecting Amy's son whom also lived in the trailer. Now three weeks after Tasha's bold move in bringing us together under Rick's roof, Rick and Amy asked for us to make different arrangements. I could see the regret in Rick's eyes and his body language told me that he really wished this wasn't the way he wished for things to turn out. I recalled that once while engaged in conversation with Rick over the last couple of weeks that he had informed me of his past mistakes including an arrest and prison sentence imposed for possession of large quantities of marijuana. He basically had said it caused him to turn his life around.

Factoring in the behavior of Tasha and I over the last weeks, I'm sure it was quite evident that we were under the influence of some heavy drug to be acting in the manner presented.

Knowing homelessness was our next step; tears welled up in my eyes. Now Tasha, myself and Charlie, my dead brother's dog, were to spend many nights in that Chevy in the vacant lots across the town.

One of those nights after driving around town warming up the car, I drove until I found an old country road. There were flurries in the air and Tasha thought to start kissing on my neck, lips and cheeks. It didn't take long for my breathing to come in quick sighs. I pulled that car over and put the seat back in a reclined position. Within hurried seconds, we were both skin on skin naked. Erotica in the wide open brings the feeling of risk that you might get just get caught. Senses peeked, writhing in gasps to the mounting tension of pleasure, the windows soon fogged over.

Though it was an old country road, vehicles would pass us by only adding to the facetiousness. Tasha nor I paid no mind. We enjoyed each other until we were spent. I can only explain how spent that as Tasha decided to crawl her way her naked self into the back seat to catch her breath but soon was fast asleep. Little Charlie was situated in the back window.

I pulled my pants back on for the had been to my ankles.

I noticed nothing as I attempted to get myself together until there was that knocking on my driver's side window. The flashlight shining bright in my eyes told me just what this was about. It was a sheriff of the county. He shown his light to the back seat and as I seen Tasha's naked ass under the beam of light my pulse soon quickened. I breathed out Tasha's name with the best of my ability due to the excitement of the arrival of the sheriff and a nagging rising need to take Tasha once again.

The officer either heard me say her name or probably knew her for in the next moment he was telling her by name to put some clothes on as if this was like some everyday occurrence.

He said, "Well, I now know what you guys have been doing, so I have the answer to that. Matthew, do you remember me? I was down at the trailer when your brother died."

I answered, "Oh".

Ya know, some people have the gift to think on their toes, but I am not one of those people. I have found that when communicating with law enforcement, it is often best to say little as possible.

The sheriff waited for Tasha to put her clothes on, turned off his flashlight, and simply stated," There is no parking on this road. Roads are icy, so drive safely." then he simply left got in his cruiser and drove away.

Over the next couple of weeks, Charlie, I and Tasha lived in that little Chevy cavalier. During the day, Tasha directed me to churches which often took us right to the gas station, purchasing us a full tank of gas for the car as well as a gas station lunch. Both Tasha and I filled out applications for the community centers in hopes of securing funds for rent and security deposits. We utilized food banks and took our meals to Rob's house rather than leave it in the trunk to become frozen and unable to be eaten easily.

When Christmas came, it was nice to be woken by a tap on the window as Rob invited us in to a hot Christmas meal.

It was Rob's full time job caring for Trinity, Tasha's daughter and these people becoming accepting of me with all my problems was where I soon found myself attached.

At the Christmas dinner, Rob told us we could stay in the spare bedroom until we found a place of our own. Needless to say, sleeping in a warm house next to a warm body was what seemed like a great luxury.

Christmas in particular gave a new light to the giving season. However the morning after, still groggy from sleep, I received a call from a pastor of the nearby church. I had left calls to many churches pleading for monetary fund's due to the fact that I was basically homeless. It was like a breathe of cool air when the pastor offered a full month's rent and security deposit for a large three bedroom heated house.

The pastor asked us to meet him at the church a near two miles away. There was no condescending attitude. The pastor gave from the heart as he stated, "there is no one in such need of help as the two of you."

We left the church with a check for fifteen hundred dollars, and a check for the deposit to have the gas and electric transferred into my name. We were also put up in a hotel for the remaining days of the month in which was necessary for we were unable to move in until the first. In my state of mind this was nothing less than a miracle.

Having our own place or our whole entire house rather, it was its own benefits. I could now rock your sox off listening to music as loud as I wanted without disturbing neighbors, the biggest advantage besides having to muffle loud sex screams that for sure were about to ensue.

I had in earlier months through employment, which by any means, was sporadic, had the made acquaintance of a girl by the name of Tara. We had met by working in a lumberyard of hardwoods. Tara and her boyfriend by the name of Chris were methamphetamine addicts. As I understood, the drug gave the needed energy to work easily at a competitive speed. The bright light appeared like a light bulb when I learned with a little practice and cleaners that could be found under most peoples kitchen sink, I could make vast amounts of this drug for cheap. The facts of the heavenly road had been brought to my attention when I received a call from Tara asking me if I was interested in some meth for cheap. "How cheap?" was my line in tow. "Fifteen bucks," was the answer that put me out the house without the girlfriend for the spell not far behind.

This was soon to be a course of continuous sales from Walgreens and the nearby hardware store. By now I had some sort of epiphany that the manufacturing of methamphetamines was a way for me to intoxicate and most probable an easy way to make money through a sale or two if I favored that decision for the day.

Due to the fact that a user of methamphetamines is most often than not a paranoid subject taking into consideration that someone any one person or who facilitates or has any knowing in the manufacturing is guilty of a felony charge by association.

This is the reason my friend in which I had interest in seeing the process of making the meth he would let no one watch him as he manufactured the drug from simple house cleaners and a couple boxes of cold medicine. With my schooling in chemistry taken from the multiple courses I took at leisure in attempt to better my life.

Well a couple days later, we learned another lesson the he hard way. Thinking the process was running smoothly, the cooking began endlessly. After the pro

One box of cold medicine every two weeks was the limit in attempt to control the flow of the processed medicine making meth.

Chris became evermore paranoid as inhalation of the drug can often. Now having a fresh house I held it like a carrot in front of a rabbit. It was a no brainer, for we had   just moved into the house; we had a long leash if only it were to hang myself. I thought of this like free drugs along with access to the easy money.

The act of cooking, the process in bonding the cellular structure tends to be the most retched smell. It is a chemical fog that saturated the air to the point that the windows must be opened or you are sure to inhale the fog which by nature will take the oxygen out the air and replace it with something on the lines of mustard gas.

In one of my first chemistry escapades, I made an error in the weights of the ingredients. I in turn had produced a form of mustard gas that suffocated Tasha and I to the point of puking bile while trying to breathe a gulp of air. Dangerous is an understatement when considering the risk involved in the manufacturing of methamphetamine.

A few weeks of manufacturing, after weeks of use I began to see aberrations. I began to see an old man walk the stairs. Footsteps could be heard walking on the floor boards of the upstairs while on the ground floor. So paralyzed by fear with the inability to physically move, there was time when one instance I thought I must have been held down by some force and a power drill was being used tobore a hole in my head. As the ringing became louder the idea of being lobotomized.

Tasha would later tell me that she had witnessed me have several seizures. She had called her mother, for she was in fear that my life may be in jeopardy. Knowing that methamphetamines coarse through my veins, it was common knowledge to never call emergency dispatch, for that would include police contact. I was later informed that Tasha made every effort and found seizure medication in which she fed me. After what seemed an eternity I closed the windows of the soul and soon found peace as I faded to rest.

Our recently acquired house was what brought me into a close relationship with her family. Tasha's mother lived directly across the alley and her younger sister, I soon learned was only a vacant lot away living with her boyfriend.

We had very little amenities of our own moving in that house. There was no refrigerator. We made the best of the winter season and stored our food on the porch which kept it frozen. This allowed us to be forced to buy smaller amounts of grocery, for the grocery store in town were complete price gougers.

Tasha and I would recuperate by filling upon most often sweets and junk food. It was the greatest attempt to fill what seemed to be the bottomless hole through your soul. We would watch the same movies as we faded into the depths of sleep to wake only to suck down a cigarette or two, always attempting with greatest intention to force fluids in order to hydrate. It was then back to the darkness not before restarting the same movie that I never seemed to see beginning to end. The surrender to sleep was the big part of the withdrawal associated methamphetamine use.

Then at a moment's notice we were either in transport to acquire the ingredients or in midst of a quick cook or being visited by the mother of Tasha in assurance and high hope that she would be given by blessing to yet to see with her eyes that yet we were still alive. It was her intent to bring us cigarettes and food. I do believe Tasha had inherited that spunk and sparkle from the genes of her mother. I did see that life force energy by notice in time spent with the little sister. Her name was Tracy but surely that is a whole other book of joy in large quantity.

I had never met individuals that were so open to nakedness. Yes, I said nakedness. As for Tasha, it was little to no effort to get her birthday suite sweat soaked. She was always out to try and make me laugh, or so it seemed. Do you really ever know a person? (Truly?) Mary, Tasha's mother, for instance, showed her face one day at the house of propriety, our ill-conceived home. She whispers something to Tasha, and the next moment she ripped up her shirt (no bra) breast and nothing but oriel, forever imprinted to memory. Tasha laughs, and all I could do is return with a look that showed a dismissal or maybe a tad disgust "What the fuck? Where the fuck did this come from?", I fired without interjection. I must have turned three sheets of red! I am completely male so I later smiled, maybe the grin a bit evil.

The family of Tasha's was a different breed. One day, visiting mother, the whole gang was in attendance. Tasha's sister, Amy, decided that due to the fact I was wearing jogging pants, she would rip them down, underwear and all. Of course, everyone but me thought it was hilarious. This included children of Tasha's sister Tracy whom blurted, "I saw Matt's junk!"

The whole family may have been completely crazy, but anytime I was in attendance of one or more of their family tree, my stomach would ache from laughter.

My companion Charlie, the little cocker-doodle of my late brother, was also witness, as in a front row seat, to the insanity yet kindness of this strange family. Charlie was loved by all. He was patient with the children. In return Charlie was a favorite for multiple hugs, belly rubs and the occasional treats, usually the sneaking of food from the children's plate of food.

One day, Tasha and I gathered all the paraphernalia we could fit in the car. The intent was to dispose of the hazardous implements due to a chronic paranoia which accompanied the use of the heavy drug. Sadly, due to lack of moral capability, we dispersed of the assortment of glass

200

bottles, beakers, tubing and remnants of the cook on the side of a country road. Well after casting the trash, I hadn't noticed that little Charlie wasn't trying to rest on my lap or trying to suck air out of an open window, which was "his thing" while in transit. As a matter of fact, Charlie wasn't in the back seat or posted looking out the back window.

I immediately turned the car around in search of my best little buddy. I drove for hours looking for that dang dog. I couldn't come to terms that I had left him behind. Charlie was my only tie to my memories of life with my deceased brother Randy. The guilt of my thoughtless actions of the whole ride pressed guilt heavily. I finally drove home.

While I was in a stink I took out my frustration out on the only person present, Tasha.

At just that minute my phone rang and it happened to be my last woman of pleasure, Brandy. I explained to her my sadness. She left me to my guilt and took on the loss with a different attitude. Brandy called the humane society, home of stray, lost dogs. She even took the drive, and as she happened to pulled into the drive way of the "pound", she witnessed some innocent soul trying his best to grab hold of a little fur ball he had somehow retained in his vehicle. As Brandy approached that little fur ball quit his growling and made a leap and a cry of happiness as Charlie caught sight of Brandy. Needless to say Brandy was my hero that day. She returned the little guy to me the next day when I drove to her home to pick up the dog.

This instance alone was a real eye opener. I was losing myself to the drugs, but I was unable to control it. I was losing my mind from lack of sleep .My mental illness was quite evident in my every movement. It's one of those things you know is happening to you but it's like seeing yourself out of body. I should have stopped the use of heavy drugs earlier but all I wanted was to feel better.

Tasha and I were just as you can imagine dead beats. We applied for work, and both found a job twenty miles away from the house we called home. For a twenty mile hike is considered appropriate for those that live in small villages and towns. We would sit together on breaks while choking down as much nicotine as possible.

On one occasion, I managed to, as I'm sure many others have done; I locked my keys in the car. I hadn't noticed this until we were exhausted from an honest day's pay. Well the options were to call the police, for in the small town community, these officers carried the tool to reach down the window and unlock any car to gain access. The other option was to give Tasha's mother Mary a call to at least bring a clothes hanger or screw driver to force our way into the vehicle. I chose both. Whoever showed up first was the idea that we would most appreciate.

So Tasha was the one to give phone call to the local police station requesting the assistance of an officer. When two squad cars drove into the lot I was noticing we may have got ourselves in quite a predicament. Both officers exited separately and walked briskly toward Tasha. Evidently Tasha had given her name requesting the officer's assistance.

The officer spoke and gave the air to suddenly turn b risk. He says, "I got good news and bad news. First I can open the door so you have your access to your keys again. Secondly, the bad news is that Tasha you have a warrant for your you are under arrest." He placed the cuffs on Tasha and ushered her into the back seat of the squad car.

I had no kind of money, so bailing Tasha out wasn't even given a second thought.

She was, however, able to get some attention from the guards which by fruition gave her the opportunity to speak with the municipal judge. The song and dance that the municipal judge must hear on a daily basis astounds me, but by luck of the Irish, it hadn't hardened his soul. A couple of hours later, Tasha were started the procedure in being released from custody.

Twenty miles away I finished up my petty chemistry for the day. After a moment my own pain threshold was bloviated, and off I flew to pick the girl up.

Being released from any county jail is not a fast process. To the officers, this job is one of the mundane chores of the day. By complete repetition, it drags on like any other job. Tasha finally walked out the doors of the county correctional institution.

As she glided bodily into the passenger seat of the car, I held out the tool filled with the drug that I was running on. It was the amphetamine I earlier had chemically manufactured.

Surprisingly, the next morning we drove our way to work, basically mind you, having had no sleep, for the legs of the drug were long. (This meaning the life of the drug would last for many hours depending on how long the user had been using.)

In the brisk morning I meandered my way out to the car to let the thing warm up as I did regularly. As I walked down the steps of the wooden porch my boot lost my stand and went right out from under me. I hit straight down on my tailbone and I let out something g that resembled a language close in sound as one would hear at an exorcism. I knew at that moment that I would catch hell of ridicule from that buoyant bitch, a woman I called mine. Tasha, I think, rolled her way down the stairs in the inside of the house. I could hear her roar of laughter seriously, for the next ten minutes. She later told me, she had heard the thud and my immediate string of curse words. She knew exactly what had transpired in those few moments. I found my left boot which had come off my foot and traveled into a snow pile twenty feet away.

Tasha and I worked the morning thru, but at the lunchtime bell we were escorted to the managing office and fired and given no cause. At a later date, a fellow employee had informed us that another employee had dropped a syringe into the garbage and it was assumed to be mine or Tasha's paraphernalia. Thus the reason we were "let go".

Chapter 35

"The only source of knowledge is experience"

-- Albert Einstein

As days passed with now none of this crystalized chemistry available for pain, for no other reason than to get information, I suddenly remembered why I was really calling her, for she had morphine pills that tend to feel real good to a guy like me. Well Tasha wasn't having it whatsoever. The temperature in the house, I swear, rose a couple degrees.

Tasha simply said, "If you leave, there will surely be someone warming your side of the bed. Don't come back!"

Without realizing I swung and connected with her skull. I swear, it wasn't my grandest moment. I realized what I had done and the guilt came flooding in. She later told me she saw stars. It took me a long time to forgive myself for that discrepancy. It wasn't before I went to get into the car and a shovel careened off the windshield. My guilt got the best of me with straight taxation.

I found my way into the house and must have apologized for hours. The next thing I know, I passed out into deep sleep wrapped in her arms.

The next waking moment, I sent Tasha down to find something to eat. Mind you she was just as exhausted as me, but when she reached the kitchen, she was in for a big surprise. The land lord was in our kitchen. If you could imagine the disaster the kitchen was in, we had lost our income, were using the winter temperatures to keep our food cold, for we had no refrigerator. The slothful tendencies that we were embellishing in made all things worse for wear. You

Well, Tasha knew the landlord quite well. In these little towns everyone knows everyone, and most likely fucked each other also. Landlord got caught and with Tasha coming to see this intrusion, I imagine it was like being wrapped around as if a snake is restricting on your sorry ass.

"What the fuck are you doing in here?" She fired. The landlord, having the name of Gary, knew he was in the wrong for entering without notice and backed up back out the door. "Really Gary what do you think you're doing?"

Gary fired back without a seconds notice, "You guys better know what it is that you're doing. You need to stop!!! This is being investigated at a state level."

Gary was well informed; so to heed his word was a wise idea. Gary owned many houses across the state, and he had credible influence through the law enforcement.

Chapter 38 as much needed rest the first thing on my mind is what is there to eat and is the front porch still cold enough to keep the food we were storing out there because we had no freezer or refrigerator of course being a cigarette smoker the second thought was do we have cigarette the specific morning Tasha and I were both awakened by the familiar banging on the back door it was Mary Tasha's mother she came bearing gifts cigarettes I don't know warm Mac and cheese Better yet she bought coffee grounds to make coffee Mary never stayed long still dazed and confused Tasha yells ******* and Mary lifts her shirt it brought laughter from my soul the family was crazy Mary excited as fast as she appeared.

A pile of dishes was the usual set in the kitchen so after smokes and bite to eat I set to washing the dishes and creating a pile of dry this would also be the time I would come through the house disabling the makeshift lab for cooking meth. Whatever could would be cut into pieces and flushed down the toilet. Within in pieces I could no longer worry about it clogged in the pipes. I would flush down the toilet the only remaining of the cook that's a bloated bottle of remains in the lab ingredients needed to be discarded but kept in mind the bathroom fire we would discard anywhere but in the toilet. After shared bath washing the other Tasha and I will once again melt back into each other 's arms. Just touching ignited a violent passion between us. The skin scraping punishment and course manhandling was today's menu after moments of deep desire unleashed escalating to the point of ecstasy the release was heavenly. Sleep would come again in the background the droning of the disc player is an ancient Kung Fu movie took the backdrop to rest.

And what seemed less than a minute that I closed my eyes the next day I'd come.new line again the familiar knock on the back door Mary was back I sort of staggered to the door still half asleep. New line I will never forget the pale complexion as she announced I hope you guys don't have any *anything in here. There are at least seven sheriffs cars and three detectives as well as a hazmat unit at the fire department a block away!

That brought reality into light in a fraction of a second the only thing I could think of was that the bottle of the spent ingredients of my last cook sitting in the open, for all to see in the kitchen on the kitchen sink. I grabbed an empty chips

207

bag and my coat Tasha in tow and casually came out the door and as best I could manage got into the car without a hitch Tasha did the same. We left the alley and with speed maneuvered the blacks leading to the main highway. New line it was only seconds later I found in my rear room mirror those seven squad cars and a trail behind us. Lights were flashing red and blue period new line We left the highway without realization that without knowing how deep the trouble ahead of us was we were still in trouble and with the appearance of the efforts of law enforcement we were in deep trouble.

I pulled to the side of the road when I looked in the mirror and guns drawn the many bodies of the Sheriff's Department were quickly advancing.

Knowing that in any cook he possibility our chemical reaction was certainly part of the danger at risk of a possible explosion. The officers kept their distance. I keep Tasha deep kiss open the car door with one hand then from the outside of my other hand also out the window I exited the car walking backwards towards the squat team that was behind us. Without a hitch Tasha did the same.

After safely in coughs the first question asked was is there anyone in the house I said yeah my dog Charlie what looked like a detective spoke into his radio breached the house no one inside i imagine Charlie was in for a surprise.

Placed in a sheriff's car Tasha and one in the other we were chauffeured back to our den of at least three months with people in what looked like space suits busy gathering under what could have been a circus tent.

Garbage bags were dumped on tables as the guys in suits picked up each item a decorated by colorful pins officer came to the back door the squad I'm with the drug test team for the for the five county area he began. I caught him off at that point when I quickly interjected one word pal's lawyer. He slammed the squad door and the officer driving me began his trek towards the county jail tasha and her own squad car followed right behind.

There are no words for the feeling of your waking moment to learn your nightmare with real and you're in jail and most likely on your way to prison freedom are not in the foreseeable future. The closest word to feeling can only be anguish.

No sooner had I been awakened and I was being led out of my cell to be brought in front of a detective. To set the scene properly Imagine a man in business attire offering the simple pleasures as in a hot cup of coffee a cigarette and some kind words.

Anyways after a cup of coffee and being taken outside to smok.The businessman took me in a small room and sit behind the table. The detective knowing of my brother's death being the same detective that lectured me at my brother's trailer after his overdose brought my loss to my mind.

Police in general are often bullies hey poke around for information and as a scare tactic they lie in order to extract information out of you any way they can.

Where a police procedure I made a small conversation with the detective and politely declined any further discussion. This was my exit strategy and it worked fine.

Within hours I was in front of a television with camera access to be heard on bail in communication with the judge.

Chapter 36

"I form the light, and create darkness: I make peace and create evil, I the lord doeth all these things."

-- Isaiah 45:7

Through the next 11 months that I was incarcerated I involve myself in a drug therapy program in which I completed I've done many in my past lifetime only to be returned to use the lessons in behavior modification. They say drug addiction is a disease because one can really never fully recover an addiction never goes away it always lives inside your mind.

While I was incarcerated Tasha's ex-husband died of an overdose. This was just another decent man taken from this world.

I met some interesting people in jail. Small towns and counties it seemed most inmates were either on a holds from parole officer have new charges. Most frequently they are all drug related. I met a kid around 20 years old later found out while under the influence of methamphetamine he had caught his friend's throat with a fillet knife. He had been up for multiple days and also stabbed the woman. I asked, "why I just stab her in the leg?", he simply answered," she was trying to get away." Later I found out that his name was Shane he had a very traumatic childhood and meth had done Its work of evil on him.

I communicated with Tasha the whole time via mail while I was incarcerated in my mind our love was growing and withstanding our troubles pleading guilty to conspiracy to manufacture meth and sentenced to probation and the understanding that further criminal activity could ultimately land me in prison for years and after completing a drug rehab program which satisfied the parole agent enough to deem society safe for me I was released back into the ocean of society.

While incarcerated a judge found me mentally disabled due to a long past of mental health issues. I was awarded Social Security income it I wasn't eligible for Social Security disability because I had never been able to stay stable long enough to keep a job building credits in the eyes of the government. The difference being I was allotted much less money to live on by hundreds of dollars.

Now yes released in that ocean of society it wasn't long before I started once again to need relief from life I was living with a woman that had taken care of Charlie like cockatoo while I was away being the only place I could find at the moment to stay at she began to notice a difference in my behavior she called my parole agent who later contacted me and I was ordered to accommodate with a urine drug screen yes I failed for meth. Being given a sanction I was processed into the county jail in attempt to clean out my system of the illicit drugs

While being processed into the jail while giving my fingerprints for the database whom do you think I bumped into it was Tasha who was working on a job release from the jail which is called Huber release being clean in the atmosphere of controlled environment she wasn't so happy to see I was back in confines so quickly

I was released after five days dry out. This allowed my physical system of the body to be free of drugs.

I didn't do so well handling the freedom for addiction never goes away because it lives within your mind meth is known to reroute neural pathways in the brain.

After only a couple of days I was using again not wishing to be around my roommates I spent most time in acquaintance named Eric. He lived with his dad and his wife Ashley had two children and after not sleeping for several days I passed out on Eric's couch I awakened to see that the my pipe used to smoke meth which is called a bubble from blown glass resembling a bubble it fell out of my hand or my pocket onto the floor or coach to be found by one of Eric's and Ashley's daughters. She was holding it in her mouth obviously she had seen this behavior before but it was the straw that broke the camel's back because I was asked to leave.

From being awake from multiple days the body literally passes into sleep without much notice.

I left Eric's house and walked to the outside stairs up Eric's father's door but fell asleep on the stairs I woke to an officer ushering me out of the gangway. Dave Eric's father had called the police. I can only imagine that act was because he believed I had no more drugs to share with him. The dismissal behavior is vindictive of many addicts after the consumption of another drugs and believing them to be broke are often quite dismissed rudely.

The officer drove me to the house in my roommate trying to maintain appearances I did my best to set up an injection to become cognizant and injection as to become cognitive for sleep threatened my coherence sleep went out I passed out before injecting the much needed fix

In this contradiction a person whose body is trying to recuperate is often in pain because of the abuse the body had during the awake.

This often causes one to moan in their sleep while their body is recuperating obviously when hurt overwhelms the body you tend to moan not even knowing so my roommate recorded this on their telephone and also called the police to do a Wellness check on me I awakened opening my eyes. The sight of a law enforcement officer brought me to reality quite quickly. The officer was pointing on the floor of the left side of the bed where syringe of crystalline substance it was harpoon to the carpet. His only words were you know you're coming with me right? At that moment I realized in my right fist was four separate packaged Baggies full of methamphetamine.

With the officers attention to the syringe on the floor I was able to drop the four bags on the right side of the bed opening my fist and letting them fall between the blanket and the wall down to the floor

If this wasn't bad enough my true roommate showed the officer the small buds of marijuana on the dryer that was in my room after an hour and a half I was tucked in for the body's recuperation in the county jail with new charges of possession of controlled substance speech possession of drug paraphernalia possession of marijuana. Nice roommates

My parole officer made me sit 60 days as another sanction for my drug use upon release I moved to a different county in an attempt to keep clean of drug use. My parole officer gave me access to temporary living quarters from the Department of Corrections to get back on my feet

In a new town I met new people. One of the people I met was named what was named Joel and he had a girlfriend named Megan I was able to rent a room from them Joel was an avid drinker and Megan would partake on weekends when she was Free from the responsibilities of work.

I never saw alcohol to be a problem on my own life. Alcohol has its benefits period it was legal and I couldn't get out of prison for drinking I couldn't get sent to prison for drinking and having a roommate Joel who enjoyed drinking much more than even I did soon we became quite good friends we were both antisocial hated people but loved to eat well and watch videos and movies while catching the bus

I was soon able to purchase a vehicle which enabled me to spend time with Tasha. Soon I was traveling hours to take her to work in the morning and traveling an hour to pick her up from work Weekends Tasha would spend time with me. I soon moved into in with Mary Tasha's mother and her boyfriend Sylvester Tasha soon also moved in I was unable to take her to work without spending an hour each way in travel time and we were soon joined at the hip

After a couple of months I asked Tasha to marry me and she accepted.

Day of our wedding we started celebrating early with a pint of cinnamon whiskey with Tasha's daughter Trinity as our ring bearer we were married in the courthouse our reception was at a friend's home it was simple completed with the smashing of Cree cake on the bride and groom's face.

Tasha and I celebrated by engaging each other in drinks at the bar where we celebrated by ourselves we rented a hotel room that was above the Tavern which included a hot tub in the room. Tasha been married and divorced prior to our relationship. I was careful and happy to make our wedding night personal for only the two of us. Tasha 's first wedding her groom rob had invited Tasha's family to the hotel room in which the story has been told that by the morning rob had to be taken to the hospital. Being deprived of the consumption of the wedding night Tasha had waited till rob fell asleep and super glued his running to his leg. New line in light of this I had been sure that our night was to be special.

Chapter 37

"It is not I who created myself, rather I happened to myself."

-- CJ Jung

Soon Tasha and I were able to move into our own house with Charlie my dog in tow.

With our own house came our own privacy. With their own privacy came drug use when I was when we couldn't afford the drugs we drank. It happened that in the course that purchased a couple of grams of methamphetamine. Snorting meth tends to burn your nostril canals smoking meth is the next in line of intensity but injecting meth is by far the most intense by intense I have come to learn that hallucinations can and will kick your sanity down the road. I have elucidated from rabie disease bats, to alligators and crocodiles to grizzly bears.

Meth is sure to spur the imagination.

Math will produce what you fear most.

On several occasions Tasha would fall asleep before I did though I would have the axis of laying with her in my mind I saw lumps the blankets and to me my imagination my schizophrenia became real I would see another body laid there next to this is Nolan among addicts often referred to as the shadow people. The dread and fearful paranoia is all consuming. For me it was the fear that made my wife was sleeping with another man. The devastation was so severe that it would at times wake her to argue it with her. I'm sure you can imagine her anger as I work her and pull her apart away from the her much needed sleep.

Bears were also a great fear of mine I have become sure of reasoning. Within the years of my life I had happened upon a documentary of a photographer that defying all odds for the while he lived among the grizzly bear.new line he photographed them in the wild for a time his girlfriend had lived with him but what I recall she grew fearful and later escaped on her own accord the photographer wasn't so lucky. After not hearing from him for a number of days game wardens found his camp torn to shreds evidence of a dramatic event.

It designed to kill an especially aggressive bear that took to the area proved that the photographer had been eaten by the bear for remains of him were found in the belly of the bear after killing it.

And one account after injecting, I imagine two baby bears wandering out from under my computer desk. In my mind my thoughts raised and sense of insanity dawned on me that where there are baby Cubs the mother was not far behind.

Tasha happened to be taking a shower at the time so the bathroom door was closed. Thinking her safe I actually did the house frantically running up the street. The back of my neck tents from the drama of the situation gripped by the muscles but soon imagined that I was being bitten the whole time I was down the street clutching my neck only to look back thinking the bear had seized me the clutching of my own neck was his bite.new line I ran for blocks, I came to a busy highway. In the state of psychosis I flagged cars down. Horns blaring I was finally able to stop a car in which I got into the back seat while the frightened lady drove about the block before stopping the car and demanding I get out of her car.new line from there I did get out of the car but the imagination now projected people conspiring to hurt me and attack me. I dashed into the gas station and begged the clerk to call the police. I must have had some sense because I recall checking my pockets to be absolutely sure I possess no drugs on my person.new line I was absolutely petrified as I looked about my surroundings period of course I was the scene so people were watching me. Next the sheriff showed up seeing my state of mind he placed me in the back of his car was seat of his car I imagine after acquiring my name and the birth date for me looked he looked on the computer and my criminal record possession of meth was probable that is what I was suffering hallucinations from. New line he decided to take me to the hospital.

Now my mental state had turned from bad to worse my mind telling me that the sheriff had a plan to execute me in the woods the ride to the hospital took about ½ hour living in rural areas this is the average time for any emergency vehicle.new line when we finally made it to the emergency room my blood pressure was very high a pulse in the frenzied state. The last thing I remember was the doctor coming upon me with the syringe stating Matthew I have to slow you down or you will die.new line I regained coherency to find myself with a cane walking in hallway in a place I didn't know I was listening to a man and the doctor's coat explained to me that he thought it was time I went home still in a daze I was escorted to the telephone where I called Tasha picked me up tasha's mother did pick me up.new line She arrived with her mother Mary sylvesters Mary's boyfriend I hogged held was held by Mary Tasha explained that they were so scared for me and that I had been gone for four days and no one knew where I was or where I had been.

If so deeply on the subject what is it that I continually use this drug when at least I experience such terrifying events? Well I I can say that after a binge waking and injecting the drug allows the brain's body to function when otherwise it would not As for continued use after initial injection is primarily a social aspect to maintain coherence but defining moments resulting in the imagination and the hallucination causing fear. I have thought long and hard I believe the survival of otherwise I'm mental death can only the only reason to use this drug.

And a binge that Tasha and I were sailing in the throes of addiction it came down to the desire for more. We had run out. With her last $20, I decided acquaintance that of a dealer in the rural country wooden could supply us another hit another fix and we could use as we exploit ourselves into sexual gratification the thralls we're just excitement.new line as I walked down the gloomy lit road I was passed by a cruiser I wouldn't listen to Tasha I needed one just one more so as the cruiser passed it was a sheriff's chief I continued my walk in a better equipped state of mind I would have thought that to be a bad omen and return home. Instead I carried on with my plan to acquire the drugs that I would use to push the wife into new heights meth stimulates the libido and enhances sexual desire I had a plan and work would not be swayed.new line After a couple of blocks of walking I cut up from the alley into the backyard of jeremy's house he opened the back door of the garage stepped into the still darkness of the garage just at that moment when I heard a gun of an automobile engine and watched through the glass of the front of the garage as that would appear that some sheriff's vehicle vehicle speed past the front of the house. In the dark Jeremy groped and found my arm then putting a plastic in my hand I knew what was what I was and I was here to acquire. I slipped in I slipped it into my mouth I'm not sure Jeremy saying do this or we were just thinking alike when he stated swallow it if you have to with that I stepped over the threshold and into again the backyard.new line I often am known to zone out any and everything I do by his own out I'm referring to the state of mind well this night after also being up for multiple days I didn't Chapter 38 as much needed rest the first thing on my mind is what is there to eat and is the front porch still cold enough to keep the food we were storing out there because we had no freezer or refrigerator of course being a cigarette smoker the second thought was do we have cigarettethe specific morning Tasha and I were both awakened by the familiar banging on the back door it was Mary toshi's mother she came bearing gifts cigarettes I don't know warm Mac and cheeseBetter yet she bought coffee grounds to make coffee Mary never stayed long still dazed and confused Tasha yells ******* and Mary lifts her shirt it brought laughter from my soul the family was crazy Mary excited excited as fast as she appeared.

A pile of dishes was the usual set in the kitchen so after smokes and bite to eat I set to washing them dishes and creating a pile of dry this would also be the time I would come through the house disabling the makeshift lab for cooking meth.Whatever Icould would be cut into pieces and flushed down the toilet. Within in pieces I could no longer worry about it clogged in the pipes. I would flush down the toilet the only remaining of the cook that's a bloated bottle of remains in the lab ingredients needed to be discarded but kept in mind the bathroom fire we would discard anywhere but in The toilet. After shared bath washing the other Tasha and I will once again melt back into each other 's arms. Just touching ignited a violent passion between us. The skin scraping punishment and course manhandling was today's menu after moments of deep desire unleashed escalating to the point of ecstasy the release was heavenly. Sleep would come again in the background the droning of the disc player is an ancient Kung Fu movie took the backdrop to rest.

And what seemed less than a minute that I closed my eyes the next day I'd come.new line again the familiar knock on the back door Mary was back I sort of staggered to the door still half asleep. New line I will never forget the pale complexion as she announced I hope you guys don't have any *anything in here. There are at least seven sheriffs cars and three detectives as well as a hazmat unit at the fire department a block away!

That brought reality into light in a fraction of a second the only thing I could think of was that the bottle of the spent ingredients of my last cook sitting in the open,for all to see in the kitchen on the kitchen sink. I grabbed an empty chips bag and my coat Tasha in tow and casually came out the door and as best I could manage got into the car without a hitch Tasha did the same. We left the alley and with speed maneuvered the blacks leading to the main highway. New line it was only seconds later I found in my rear room mirror those seven squad cars and a trail behind us. Lights were flashing red and blue period new line We left the highway without realization that without knowing how deep the trouble ahead of us was we were still in trouble and with the appearance of the efforts of law enforcement we were in deep trouble.new line I pulled to the side of the road when I looked in the mirror and guns drawn the many bodies of the Sheriff's Department were quickly advancing.

Knowing that in any cook he possibility our chemical reaction was certainly part of the danger at risk of a possible explosion. The officers kept their distance. I keep Tasha deep kiss open the car door with one hand then from the outside of my other hand also out the window I exited the car walking backwards towards the squat team that was behind us. Without a hitch toshi did the same.

After safely in coughs the first question asked was is there anyone in the house I said yeah my dog Charlie what looked like a detective spoke into his radio breached the house no one inside i imagine charlie Was in for a surprise.

Placed in a sheriff's car Tasha and one in the other we were chauffeured back to our den of at least three months with people in what looked like space suits busy gathering under what could have been a circus tent.

Garbage bags were dumped on tables as the guys in suits picked up each item a decorated by colorful pins officer came to the back door the squad I'm with the drug test team for the for the five county area he began. I caught him off at that point when I quickly interjected one word pal's lawyer. He slammed the squad door and the officer driving me began his trek towards the county jail tasha and her own squad car followed right behind.

There is no words for the feeling of your waking moment to learn your nightmare with real and you're in jail and most likely on your way to prison freedom is not in the foreseeable future. The closest word to feeling can only be anguish.

No sooner had I been awakened and I was being led out of my cell to be brought in front of a detective. To set the scene properly Imagine a man in business attire offering the simple pleasures as in a hot cup of coffee a cigarette and some kind words.

Anyways after a cup of coffee and being taken outside to smok.The businessman took me in a small room and sit behind the table. The detective knowing of my brother's death being the same detective that lectured me at my brother's trailer after his overdose brought my loss to my mind.

Police in general are often bullies hey poke around for information and as a scare tactic they lie in order to extract information out of you any way they can.

Where a police procedure I made a small conversation with the detective and politely declined any further discussion. This was my exit strategy and it worked fine.

Within hours I was in front of a television with camera access to be heard on bail in communication with the judge..

I communicated with Tasha the whole time via mail while I was incarcerated in my mind our love was growing and withstanding our troubles pleading guilty to conspiracy to manufacture meth and sentenced to probation and the understanding that further criminal activity could ultimately land me in prison for years and after completing a drug rehab program which satisfied the parole agent enough to deem society safe for me I was released back into the ocean of society.

While incarcerated a judge found me mentally disabled due to a long past of mental health issues. I was awarded Social Security income it I wasn't eligible for Social Security disability because I had never been able to stay stable long enough to keep a job building credits in the eyes of the government. The difference being I was allotted much less money to live on by hundreds of dollars .

Now yes released in that ocean of society it wasn't long before I started once again to need relief from life I was living with a woman that had taken care of Charlie like cockatoo while I was away being the only place I could find at the moment to stay at she began to notice a difference in my behavior she called my parole agent who later contacted me and I was ordered to accommodate with a urine drug screen yes yes I failed for meth.

Being given a sanction I was processed into the county jail in attempt to clean out my system of the illicit drugs

While being processed into the jail while giving my fingerprints for the database whom do you think I bumped into it was Tasha who was working on a job release from the jail which is called Huber release being clean in the atmosphere of controlled environment she wasn't so happy to see I was back in confines so quickly

I was released after five days dry out. Which allowed my physical system of the body to be free of drugs new paragraph I didn't do so well handling the freedom addiction never goes away because it lives within your mind meth is known to reroute neural pathways in the brain.new paragraph After only a couple of days I was using again not wishing to be around my roommates I spent most time in acquaintance named Eric. He lived with his dad and his wife Ashley had two children and after not sleeping for several days I passed out on eric's couch I awakened to see that the my pipe used to smoke meth which is called a bubble from blown glass resembling a bubble it fell out of my hand or my pocket onto the floor or coach to be found by one of eric's and Ashley's daughters. She was holding it in her mouth obviously she had seen this behavior before but it was the straw that broke the camel's back because I was asked to leave.Paragraph

From being awake from multiple days the body literally passes into sleep without much notice.

I left eric's house and walked to the outside stairs up eric's father's door but fell asleep on the stairs I woke to an officer ushering me out of the gangway. Dave eric's father had called the police. I can only imagine that act was because he believed I had no more drugs to share with him. The dismissal behavior is vindictive of many addicts after the consumption of another drugs and believing them to be broke are often quite dismissed rudely.

The officer drove me to the house in my roommate trying to maintain appearances I did my best to set up an injection to become cognizant and injection as to become cognitive for sleep threatened my coherence sleep went out I passed out before injecting the much needed fix

In this contradiction a person whose body is trying to recuperate is often in pain because of the abuse the body had during the awake.. new line this often causes one to moan in their sleep while their body is recuperating obviously when hurt overwhelms the body you tend to moan not even knowing so my roommate recorded this on their telephone and also called the police to do a Wellness check on me I awakened opening my eyes. The sight of a law enforcement officer brought me to reality quite quickly. The officer was pointing on the floor of the left side of the bed where syringe of crystalline substance it was harpoon to the carpet. His only words were you know you're coming with meright? At that moment I realized in my right fist

225

was four separate packaged Baggies full of methamphetamine.

With the officers attention to the syringe on the floor I was able to drop the four bags on the right side of the bed opening my fist and letting them fall between the blanket and the wall down to the floor

If this wasn't bad enough my true roommate showed the officer the small buds of marijuana on the dryer that was in my room. After an hour and a half I was tucked in for the body's recuperation in the county jail with new charges of possession of controlled substance speech possession of drug paraphernalia possession of marijuana. Nice roommates

My parole officer made me sit 60 days as another sanction for my drug use upon release I moved to a different county in an attempt to keep clean of drug use. My parole officer gave me access to a temporary living quarters from the Department of Corrections to get back on my feet.new line In a new town I met new people. One of the people I met was named what was named Joel and he had a girlfriend named Megan I was able to rent A room from them Joel was an avid drinker and Megan would partake on weekends when she was Free from the responsibilities of work.

I never saw alcohol to be a problem on my own life. Alcohol has its benefits period it was legal and I couldn't get out of prison for drinking I couldn't get sent to prison for drinking and having a roommate Joel who enjoyed drinking much more than even I did soon we became quite good friends we were both antisocial hated people but loved to eat well and watch videos and movies while catching the bus

I was soon able to purchase a vehicle which enabled me to spend time with Tasha. Soon I was traveling hours to take her to work in the morning and traveling an hour to pick her up from work.new line Weekends Tasha would spend time with me. I soon moved into in with Mary tasha's mother and her boyfriend Sylvester Tasha soon also moved in I was unable to take her to work without spending an hour each way in travel time and we were soon joined at the hip.new line after a couple of months I asked Tasha to marry me and she accepted.

Day of our wedding we started celebrating early with a pint of cinnamon whiskey with tasha's daughter Trinity as our ring bearer we were married in the courthouse our reception was at a friend's home it was simple completed with the smashing of Cree cake on the bride and groom's face.

Tasha and I celebrated by engaging each other in drinks at the bar where we celebrated by ourselves we rented a hotel room that was above the Tavern which included a hot tub in the room. Tasha been married and divorced prior to our relationship. I was careful and happy to make our wedding night personal for only the two of us. Tasha 's first wedding her groom rob had invited natasha's family to the hotel room in which the story has been told that by the morning rob had to be taken to the hospital. Being bit prived of the consumption of the wedding night tasha had waited till rob fell asleep and super glued his running to his leg. New line in light of this I had been sure that our night was to be special.

Chapter 38

There is no words for the feeling of your waking moment to learn your nightmare with real and you're in jail and most likely on your way to prison freedom is not in the foreseeable future. The closest word to feeling can only be anguish.

No sooner had I been awakened and I was being led out of my cell to be brought in front of a detective. To set the scene properly Imagine a man in business attire offering the simple pleasures as in a hot cup of coffee a cigarette and some kind words.

Anyways after a cup of coffee and being taken outside to smok.The businessman took me in a small room and sit behind the table. The detective knowing of my brother's death being the same detective that lectured me at my brother's trailer after his overdose brought my loss to my mind.

Police in general are often bullies hey poke around for information and as a scare tactic they lie in order to extract information out of you any way they can.

Where a police procedure I made a small conversation with the detective and politely declined any further discussion. This was my exit strategy and it worked fine.

Within hours I was in front of a television with camera access to be heard on bail in communication with the judge.

Chapter 39

Through the next 11 months that I was incarcerated I involve myself in a drug therapy program in which I completed I've done many in my past lifetime only to be returned to use the lessons in behavior modification. They say drug addiction is a disease because one can really never fully recover an addiction never goes away it always lives inside your mind.

whoWhile I was incarcerated toss's ex-husband died when overdose. This was just another decent man taken from this world.

I'm not some interesting people in jail small towns and counties it seemed most inmates were either on a holds from parole officer have new charges most frequently they are all drug related. I met a kid around 20 years old later found out while under the influence of methamphetamine he had caught his friend's throat with a toy fillet knife he had been up for multiple days and also stabbed the woman I asked why I just stab her he simply answered she was trying to get away later found out that his name was Shane he had a very traumatic childhood and meth had done Its work of evil on him.

I communicated with Tasha the whole time via mail while I was incarcerated in my mind our love was growing and withstanding our troubles pleading guilty to conspiracy to manufacture meth and sentenced to probation and the understanding that further criminal activity could ultimately land me in prison for years and after completing a drug rehab program which satisfied the parole agent enough to deem society safe for me I was released back into the ocean of society.

While incarcerated a judge found me mentally disabled due to a long past of mental health issues. I was awarded Social Security income it I wasn't eligible for Social Security disability because I had never been able to stay stable long enough to keep a job building credits in the eyes of the government. The difference being I was allotted much less money to live on by hundreds of dollars.

Now yes released in that ocean of society it wasn't long before I started once again to need relief from life I was living with a woman that had taken care of Charlie like cockatoo while I was away being the only place I could find at the moment to stay at she began to notice a difference in my behavior she called my parole agent who later contacted me and I was ordered to accommodate with a urine drug screen yes I failed for meth.

Being given a sanction I was processed into the county jail in attempt to clean out my system of the illicit drugs

While being processed into the jail while giving my fingerprints for the database whom do you think I bumped into it was Tasha who was working on a job release from the jail which is called Huber release being clean in the atmosphere of controlled environment she wasn't so happy to see I was back in confines so quickly

I was released after five days dry out. Which allowed my physical system of the body to be free of drugs new paragraph I didn't do so well handling the freedom addiction never goes away because it lives within your mind meth is known to reroute neural pathways in the brain.new paragraph After only a couple of days I was using again not wishing to be around my roommates I spent most time in acquaintance named Eric. He lived with his dad and his wife Ashley had two children and after not sleeping for several days I passed out on eric's couch I awakened to see that the my pipe used to smoke meth which is called a bubble from blown glass resembling a bubble it fell out of my hand or my pocket onto the floor or coach to be found by one of eric's and Ashley's daughters. She was holding it in her mouth obviously she had seen this behavior before but it was the straw that broke the camel's back because I was asked to leave.Paragraph

From being awake from multiple days the body literally passes into sleep without much notice.

I left Eric's house and walked to the outside stairs up Eric's father's door but fell asleep on the stairs I woke to an officer ushering me out of the gangway. Dave Eric's father had called the police. I can only imagine that act was because he believed I had no more drugs to share with him. The dismissal behavior is vindictive of many addicts after the consumption of another drugs and believing them to be broke are often quite dismissed rudely.

The officer drove me to the house in my roommate trying to maintain appearances I did my best to set up an injection to become cognizant and injection as to become cognitive for sleep threatened my coherence sleep went out I passed out before injecting the much needed fix

In this contradiction a person whose body is trying to recuperate is often in pain because of the abuse the body had during the awake.. new line this often causes one to moan in their sleep while their body is recuperating obviously when hurt overwhelms the body you tend to moan not even knowing so my roommate recorded this on their telephone and also called the police to do a Wellness check on me I awakened opening my eyes. The sight of a law enforcement officer brought me to reality quite quickly. The officer was pointing on the floor of the left side of the bed where syringe of crystalline substance it was harpoon to the carpet. His only words were you know you're coming with meright? At that moment I realized in my right fist was four separate packaged Baggies full of methamphetamine.

With the officers attention to the syringe on the floor I was able to drop the four bags on the right side of the bed opening my fist and letting them fall between the blanket and the wall down to the floor.

If this wasn't bad enough my true roommate showed the officer the small buds of marijuana on the dryer that was in my room. After an hour and a half I was tucked in for the body's recuperation in the county jail with new charges of possession of controlled substance speech possession of drug paraphernalia possession of marijuana. Nice roommates

My parole officer made me sit 60 days as another sanction for my drug use upon release I moved to a different county in an attempt to keep clean of drug use. My parole officer gave me access to a temporary living quarters from the Department of Corrections to get back on my feet.new line In a new town I met new people. One of the people I met was named what was named Joel and he had a girlfriend named Megan I was able to rent A room from them Joel was an avid drinker and Megan would partake on weekends when she was Free from the responsibilities of work.

I never saw alcohol to be a problem on my own life. Alcohol has its benefits period it was legal and I couldn't get out of prison for drinking I couldn't get sent to prison for drinking and having a roommate Joel who enjoyed drinking much more than even I did soon we became quite good friends we were both antisocial hated people but loved to eat well and watch videos and movies while catching the bus

I was soon able to purchase a vehicle which enabled me to spend time with Tasha. Soon I was traveling hours to take her to work in the morning and traveling an hour to pick her up from work.new line Weekends Tasha would spend time with me. I soon moved into in with Mary tasha's mother and her boyfriend Sylvester Tasha soon also moved in I was unable to take her to work without spending an hour each way in travel time and we were soon joined at the hip.new line after a couple of months I asked Tasha to marry me and she accepted.

Day of our wedding we started celebrating early with a pint of cinnamon whiskey with tasha's daughter Trinity as our ring bearer we were married in the courthouse our reception was at a friend's home it was simple completed with the smashing of Cree cake on the bride and groom's face.

Tasha and I celebrated by engaging each other in drinks at the bar where we celebrated by ourselves we rented a hotel room that was above the Tavern which included a hot tub in the room. Tasha been married and divorced prior to our relationship. I was careful and happy to make our wedding night personal for only the two of us. Tasha 's first wedding her groom rob had invited Tasha's family to the hotel room in which the story has been told that by the morning rob had to be taken to the hospital. Being deprived of the consumption of the wedding night Tasha had waited till rob fell asleep and super glued his running to his leg. New line in light of this I had been sure that our night was to be special.

Chapter 40

Soon Tasha and I were able to move into our own house with Charlie my dog in tow.

With our own house came our own privacy. With their own privacy came drug use when I was when we couldn't afford the drugs we drank. It happened that in the course that purchased a couple of grams of methamphetamine. Snorting meth tends to burn your nostril canals smoking meth is the next in line of intensity but injecting meth is by far the most intense by intense I have come to learn that hallucinations can and will kick your sanity down the road. I have elucidated from rabie disease bats, to alligators and crocodiles to grizzly bears.

Meth is sure to spur the imagination.

Math will produce what you fear most.

On several occasions Tasha would fall asleep before I did though I would have the axis of laying with her in my mind I saw lumps the blankets and to me my imagination my schizophrenia became real I would see another body laid there next to this is Nolan among addicts often referred to as the shadow people. The dread and fearful paranoia is all consuming. For me it was the fear that made my wife was sleeping with another man. The devastation was so severe that it would at times wake her to argue it with her. I'm sure you can imagine her anger as I work her and pull her apart away from the her much needed sleep.

Bears were also a great fear of mine I have become sure of reasoning. Within the years of my life I had happened upon a documentary of a photographer that defying all odds for the while he lived among the grizzly bear.new line he photographed them in the wild for a time his girlfriend had lived with him but what I recall she grew fearful and later escaped on her own accord the photographer wasn't so lucky. After not hearing from him for a number of days game wardens found his camp torn to shreds evidence of a dramatic event.

It designed to kill an especially aggressive bear that took to the area proved that the photographer had been eaten by the bear for remains of him were found in the belly of the bear after killing it.

And one account after injecting, I imagine two baby bears wandering out from under my computer desk. In my mind my thoughts raised and sense of insanity dawned on me that where there are baby Cubs the mother was not far behind.

Tasha happened to be taking a shower at the time so the bathroom door was closed. Thinking her safe I actually did the house frantically running up the street. The back of my neck tents from the drama of the situation gripped by the muscles but soon imagined that I was being bitten the whole time I was down the street clutching my neck only to look back thinking the bear had seized me the clutching of my own neck was his bite.new line I ran for blocks, I came to a busy highway. In the state of psychosis I flagged cars down. Horns blaring I was finally able to stop a car in which I got into the back seat while the frightened lady drove about the block before stopping the car and demanding I get out of her car.new line from there I did get out of the car but the imagination now projected people conspiring to hurt me and attack me. I dashed into the gas station and begged the clerk to call the police. I must have had some sense because I recall checking my pockets to be absolutely sure I possess no drugs on my person.new line I was absolutely petrified as I looked about my surroundings period of course I was the scene so people were watching me. Next the sheriff showed up seeing my state of mind he placed me in the back of his car was seat of his car I imagine after acquiring my name and the birth date for me looked he looked on the computer and my criminal record possession of meth was probable that is what I was suffering hallucinations from. New line he decided to take me to the hospital.

Now my mental state had turned from bad to worse my mind telling me that the sheriff had a plan to execute me in the woods the ride to the hospital took about ½ hour living in rural areas this is the average time for any emergency vehicle.new line when we finally made it to the emergency room my blood pressure was very high a pulse in the frenzied state. The last thing I remember was the doctor coming upon me with the syringe stating Matthew I have to slow you down or you will die. I regained coherency to find myself with a cane walking in hallway in a place I didn't know I was listening to a man and the doctor's coat explained to me that he thought it was time I went home still in a daze I was escorted to the telephone where I called Tasha picked me up Tasha's mother did pick me up. She arrived with her mother Mary, Sylvester, Mary's boyfriend. I was held was held by Mary. Tasha explained that they were so scared for me and that I had been gone for four days and no one knew where I was or where I had been.

I thought so deeply on the subject, what is it that I continually use this drug when at least, I experience such terrifying events? Well I can say that after a binge waking and injecting the drug allows the brain's body to function when otherwise it would not. As for continued use after initial injection is primarily a social aspect to maintain coherence but defining moments resulting in the imagination and the hallucination causing fear. I have thought long and hard I believe the survival of otherwise I'm mental. A fascination with death can be the only reason to use this drug. And a binge that Tasha and I were sailing in the throes of addiction it came down to the desire for more. We had run out. With her last $20, I decided acquaintance that of a dealer in the rural country wooden could supply us another hit another fix and we could use as we exploit ourselves into sexual gratification the thralls we're just excitement.

As I walked down the gloomy lit road I was passed by a cruiser I wouldn't listen to Tasha I needed one just one more so as the cruiser passed it was a sheriff's chief I continued my walk in a better equipped state of mind I would have thought that to be a bad omen and return home. Instead I carried on with my plan to acquire the drugs that I would use to push the wife into new heights meth stimulates the libido and enhances sexual desire I had a plan and work would not be swayed. After a couple of blocks of walking I cut up from the alley into the backyard of Jeremy's house he opened the back door of the garage stepped into the still darkness of the garage just at that moment when I heard a gun of an automobile engine and watched through the glass of the front of the garage as that would appear that some sheriff's vehicle speed past the front of the house. In the dark Jeremy groped and found my arm then putting a plastic in my hand I knew what was what I was and I was here to acquire. I slipped in I slipped it into my mouth I'm not sure Jeremy saying do this or we were just thinking alike when he stated swallow it if you have to with that I stepped over the threshold and into again the backyard.

I often am known to zone out any and everything I do. By zoning out I'm referring to the state of mind. Well this night after also being up for multiple days I didn't ocean of thoughts on my mind I was walking.

I was walking back to my house not paying attention, kind of like kicking rocks. A vehicle passed on my right. It was just as I was passing the driver's door then I noticed the black on the gray. The letters spelled Sherriff and I realized the door opened and I was being hailed. "Matt stop," he said. I recognized his voice. As I turned around, I couldn't help but notice it was the officer that had pulled me over a couple months prior for drunk driving under the influence. This must have been the sheriff that had passed me earlier. The same officer that had been shining his spotlight down the alleys was the same sheriff that had been driving around the area definitely on some ********. That's the difference between police in the rural areas and the ones in the city, the officers in the rural areas seem to me to be pettier for what was I doing so wrong that by walking in the street he needed to question what I was doing? Anyways.

Well this cop, we will call his name Joe for reference, ordered me to assume the position. This meant he wanted to search me. We went through the motions. He checked my shoes after I kicked them off, he checked my waistband. He showed his light in my face and told me to open my mouth. The bag I had required from the dealer was in my mouth. With my tongue, I tuck the package between my gum and cheek. He's shown his light in my mouth. He grabbed me by the throat and I knew he had seen it. I pushed him off of me. I tried to suck some saliva from whatever gland it came from I swallowed and Joe knew it was gone. He slammed me against the sheriff's vehicle and slapped the cuffs on me. He grabbed his walkie-talkie and signaled another officer to the scene. "He swallowed the drug. He needs emergency transport." He cried into the mic.

Within minutes another sheriff vehicle pulled out of the darkness. Officer Joe had some words with the officer then he placed me in the back of the vehicle and the car sped down the street with me in it.

Between the two of them they must have thought I swallowed a bunch. The officer turned to interrogate me from the front seat talking through the partition, "How much did you swallow? He asked. I said, "I don't know what the **** you're talking about. As if I really believe this cop was so concerned over me he had his lights on telling me I will have to have you to the hospital in 10 minutes.

When we made it to the hospital that little $20 bag I'd swallowed it was coursing through my system. I was feeling like 1,000,000 bucks even though I knew I could very well be on my way to jail.

Upon arriving at the hospital I was escorted into the emergency room I seated myself in the bed or gurney, to be examined. The doctor came in and immediately asked, "Did you swallow any drugs?" He was shining the light in my eyes. At the same time period, I simply ushered, "No Sir." The officer wasn't in the room. He tried to impress upon the doctor to order that my stomach be pumped to retrieve the drugs. This is where I had had enough. Knowing that at least this, I was in control of my medical treatment, I said I'm not allowing this. There is no cause for this. He could do nothing further for all appearances I was cognitive and I guess enough to be aware that any treatment must be within my consent. I was once again secured in handcuffs and escorted back to the squad car.

Upon reaching the county jail, in the course of my processing along which meant that I was going to be forced to stay in custody, I was interjected in reference to what I must have swallowed. After being badgered for what seemed to be hours I was placed into a single cell for observation and to be held until I was seen in front of a judge.

Two days later my parole officer came to the jail asking me for my statement of what had transpired. I explained that earlier in the day I had had methamphetamines which accounted for the drugs in my system. When you ordered me to take a urine test I went on to state the officer was harassing me and I don't know why he believes I swallowed evidence in my possession.

He left me to the return to the isolation and the observation cell it was then that sheer depression set in. The knowledge that a criminal charge could be the defining point to my violation of my parole; and with my parole revoked I would be sent back to prison to spend no less than five years behind bars away from family friends and loved ones.

Two days later I was ushered in front of the judge. All charges have been dropped for lack of evidence.

Those charges were dropped; my parole agent proceeded with the sanction of 60 more days to stay in the county jail due to my failed drug test. I believe that my agent believed the officer story of my deliberate behavior swallowing the drugs to avoid criminal charges. Because I never made a statement to the sheriff's indicating an attempt to obstruct justice there was no charges for there was no law I had broken. The only thing to scare me, where the grounds to be revoked.

Tasha opened an account to allow me to call her on the cell phone which I was incarcerated for a 60 day sanction.

I met another subject of interest during my last 10 days of my stay in the jail. I had never met a Southern man, who was to practice of voodoo,. Knowing little of the belief, and yet the practice of religion, I became intrigued. I came to believe and completely understand it is under faith that the practice becomes a life of its own. This offender was placed in a locked cell three doors down from my cell. It came to be that we would talk to each other through the air ventilation vents. It was the darkness and ignorance of the religion that intrigued me most. We talked for hours. It became a shock to me that I was told at a later date that our conversations were often seemed as language and tongues I had never noticed.

Yes, I was just as skeptical until I was informed late in the night which I was always asleep, it was after my release that I heard in the news this man had been tried. He used his wife in a voodoo practice of sacrifice.

The day of my release, I was picked up from the jail by my mother-in-law Mary's sister. She happened to live in the town and was only blocks from the jail. After a couple of hours at her home, Tasha was dropped off. After the fear that my life could have been changed so drastically had the parole agent had his way. I was so extremely happy to hold her in my arms though what would soon transpire I had never seen coming.

Chapter 41

"Find a job you love and you will never work a day in your life"

Mark Twain

And it's such a pleasant night I happily made love to my wife. I wasn't taking for granted any second of the soft caresses. I was soon off to sleep.

The next morning I began to take stock of bills and the cleanliness of the house. The counter was full of dirty dishes. There were dishes in the oven. The cupboards were bare. Besides a couple of canned beets there was no food. The bills had not been paid either.

This didn't say anything more and Tasha was most likely annihilated most of our time apart. It was no surprise for I knew how bad I myself had fallen before I learned I had to be responsible at some point or live without a roof over my head.

Before I could mentally digest our situation Tasha made me aware that she wanted her friend to come over. It was because he would buy her beer and most likely get us high, for he was in possession of methamphetamines. The thought of meth and having experienced the consequences most recently gave me the reprieve to voice I was not interested in getting high however the thought was in her head. My mouth was watering.

She made the arrangements encouraging the axe to follow.

For no other reason than a gut feeling, I asked a simple question. "Before he gets here, is there anything I need to know?" "No," she fired back. This guy that found his way to our door, when he arrived he was only a kid" By a kid I meant it was between his twenty to thirties. What happened next would be burned in my head for along time.

This dude maneuvered through the kitchen and seemed to have his sights set on the recliner in the

living room. As he took off his jacket, there was no mistaking, he was wearing my clothes." I like that

shirt." I think he's seen this registering in my mind. His next statement was: "I've been screwing your

wife for the last two months."

I steadied my heart. I calmly stated, "I like that shirt better, and I traded shirts with him. Next, I grabbed

a beer. Nothing much knowing what to do except to run with it, I sat back and watched my wife interact

with this kid like I wasn't there.

Before long, we all drank what he had brought over. So Tasha and her boyfriend, boy toy headed to the

store walking.

Whether it was my imagination or bare truth, when they returned arm in arm, I could swear there was

grass in her hair and dirt on her knees. That was enough!

"Pack your **** and get out!!" were the words that came next ,so that's what she did.

After she had left, my eyes we're wide open to the obvious struggle she had undertaken while I was

away. All the dishes were dirty they were piled in the sink and stuck and hidden from sight in the stove

and even thrown in the backyard.

There was a zero balance on my debit card and it was only the 9 th of the month. I would have to wait

until the next month before I would have any cash. The bills hadn't been paid and upon inspecting what

was to be my rations for food I looked in the cupboards, and found them bare but for a couple cans of

beets.

The impact of the depression to follow was life shattering. I called Mary my mother-in-law multiple

times a day often full of tears wetting my face and trembling from trauma. In this next evening I filled

the bathtub with warm water. After I was nude I slipped on in that warmth. My soul to bear I took the

steak knife I had placed on the flat of the tub and I cut and I cut till the blood ran. Exhausted I drifted to

sleep giving up my soul.

When I awoke I was in blood tainted water. I have no understanding of why life had not left me .It is my

understanding I must not have cut deep enough.

In that moment all things changed I knew that there could only be purpose for life in me. Though the

sadness still remained like an ache in my heart the pain had been taken away.

I ate very little for the next month. I found a couple of gallons of paint in the basement began to clean

the walls in one room at a time.

Chapter 42

"In the beginning was the Word, and the Word was with God and the Word was God"

--- John 1:1

With my last incarceration, I had met a man named Nick who got himself arrested while passed out in the park. He had been arrested for drunk driving. The bartender refused to serve Nick, he was asked to leave for his state of intoxication was more than the trouble of another drink.

The bartender had called police when he watched Nick drive his truck away.

It turned out after a moment behind the wheel Nick realized he was in no condition to drive and had abandoned his vehicle and on his long walk home decided to stop and rest at the park. Parks close at 10:00 o'clock and it was 12:00 o'clock. It was unfortunate for Nick to be arrested that evening, but in all honesty he later told me he probably would have died because of the temperature was below freezing.

Due to Nick's incarceration, he had lost his roof over his head, for he had a mischievous girlfriend who spent every dime of his.

After my incarceration, I called him. I found that he was living in a hotel much above his means. We hung out regularly. It was running the errands and for me it was an escape from the solitude and idleness of being home alone.

Nick has having a hard time finding a rental and the fact that I didn't much like being alone in the house

I offered Nick's living space in the basement of the house in so much he accepted gladly.

Before long I was back to my old ways I purchased a large amount of methamphetamine for use and as with any drug if you possess it people will come from far and wide to buy it as fast as you can obtain it.

In the moment an unavoidable fact surfaced. It was for me to ponder. My actions were creating a real risky situation. My possession, let alone sales and use of the drug, if I was to ever be caught would send me back to prison without a doubt. This wasn't a matter of if. It was only a matter of when.

I guess you could call me a gambler. I threw caution to the wind and at that defining moment life seemed to brim full of possibilities. I think it may have just been the drug talking.

It took a moment for people to know that I possessed a substantial amount of drugs at any time but this was certainly a means to an end.

As with any drug if you possess it people will buy it as fast as you can obtain it.

In this moment an unavoidable facts surfaced for me to ponder. My actions were creating a real risky situation. My possession let alone sales and use of the drug if I was ever caught would send me back to prison without a doubt.

I guess you could call me a gambler. I threw caution to the wind and at that defining moment is when life began to explode like propulsion.

It took a moment for people to know that I possessed it, and I possessed a substantial amount of drugs and with a kind soul empathized with others who had a daily habit. I had no problem helping them out from time to time but with the loan of this product that made me quite the list of clientele.

Money was easy to come by. More often than not it was easy come easy go.There was even a time or two I sent cash to women I had met on the Internet.

After thinking about it a spell later I came to the hard facts that I had probably sent my money to some dude posing as a woman. It's amazing how foolish one could be in the thralls of loneliness. It wasn't long before there were women that would show up with no money.

Methamphetamines is a drug that when used you can find most anything to do and become obsessed in doing whatever may have been interesting at that moment. It wasn't out of the realms of belief that a woman would come over with the intent to socialize. This often led to sexual stimulation and of course sex and then it was off to another project.

Often I would ask people to clean the house. One girl named Ashley, while I

caught up in a couple of hours of sleep, had completely broken down every part of the living room and kitchen even to the removal of the blinds for soaking and rearrange the whole living room. At first when I woke I seen the house in shambling. I, grumbling with the thought that I would be the one having to put the place back together, fell back off to sleep. I woke a couple hours later with the house clean from top to bottom.

It must be understood that this is so different than Tasha who left dishes till there was no clean dishes and it was her to wash a single item just for that one bite to eat.

Methamphetamines are known to stimulate the libido. Sex often lasting at one memorable adventure lasted 10 hours. Multiple partners at the same occasion were nothing I would run from if ever came into fruition.

When the time came, which were many, that I hadn't taken my medication or had to deprive myself of sleep for extensive periods bringing about hallucinations.Nick was there to bring me back to some semblance of sanity. On one occasion while I was in a moment of terror hallucinating black bears in the living room Nick was the voice of reason distracting my attention with semantics such as naming and counting these objects of my state. There were times also then Nick would grow tired of having to be the voice of reason and inflict his own type of psychological terror. I guess we all have our dark side.

The constant threat of an encounter with law enforcement was taxing. Law enforcement in the rural countryside is much different than in the city. It would seem due to less people an officer in the country will often run the plates of a car that is parked on the side of the road, for instance parked outside of a tavern.

Now armed with the information as an individual's background in officer will stop a vehicle armed with an agenda. It isn't unheard of that an officer will run the registration of vehicle passing in the opposite direction creating a cause for suspicion resulting in a traffic stop.

Person such as I with a background of drug abuse now becomes the object of fixation. An officer will often lie in wait such as a leaving my home to be followed from my residence pulled over to have an officer run a drug dog through my vehicle to see if an arrest can be made.

The officer Joe was consistent in his monitoring of my actions. So one could see how the threat that hovers in possession of a street drug such as meth, which has been pictured in society as an epidemic which carries stiff penalties of incarceration often for extensive periods of time.

If there is suspicion of a drug activity which is pretty much automatic when an officer sees a criminal record such as mine which includes drug charges beginning as a span of 30 years. The officer will often search the vehicle during a stop, but if there is a canine unit in the area or available, the dog will go over the vehicle with its keen sense of smell. Were to be carrying a smelling salt used to bring an unconscious body into consciousness the intense scent of ammonia will deteriorate dark sense of smell for about an hour. I could carry a small bottle of ammonia the splash around the vehicle if I am to believe that that canine search was to ensue.

Some officers are shipped to this deterrent and are not too happy if they catch on. It is just best not to transport paraphernalia such as pipes or water pipes scales for accuracy and in purchasing large quantities or multiple bags to distribute product or obviously about any amount of drug especially pertaining to methamphetamines. When dealing in sales of drugs it is not a question of "if "you will be arrested but" when";. It is a known fact that most often an individual who has been arrested will set up controlled buys of illegal drugs by wearing a camera or listening device in order to have an agent of the law reduce the charges or allow the District Attorney to be informed that one has been cooperative. The threat of being slipped off into prison is often all it takes before many inform on a dealer known to them.

Chapter 43

The windows were rolled down. I was tired. My senses seemed peaked but dull. My body was demanding a full night's rest food and a quiet atmosphere. My body demanded retreat. I had just sneaked away from the couple's house my body would get it to rest for the blackness that was enveloping around me. I had to get away from the evil of men's mind.

That man was dressed as a woman yellow billowing gown with a man's berth. To each their own. I dare not even dream of what the hell he would find seductive. I had just left without noise I could hear them. I could hear her advances to anyone who would listen. The cons. She is the reason I had to vacate. Better just to get home with my wallet intact. A con will always strike when you're weak sleeping or yet in a psychotic state which I had begun to have many.

On an old country road, I maneuvered the domestic soccer moms van. The speed that felt adequate for the mood I was in. It was a thrill. I pushed the gas pedal that increased the speed. The rest of the evening that would be mine oh so I thought.

I took the left hand turn on the Carl St. My home was three houses in from the corner. I could see the driveway but by the porch light. I pulled into my lot and hit the brakes the front brakes squeaked a bit. I put the van in the park.

A Jeep looking type vehicle pulled off to my right I could barely see him as he flipped on his lights and pulled behind me.

My adrenaline surged: ammonia smelling salts, get to the door!

Chapter 44

"Great and marvelous are thy works, O Lord God the Almighty"

Revelations 15:3

Knowing that at this time in my life I was going to be revoked my parole that's a 10 year sentence plus up to seven for the possession charge and that was concurrent on parole for that now, this charge for habitual criminality that's not to mention if I'm charged for the third operating after restricted substance a possible 27 years erasing all friendships marriage was going to go to shit. This put the icing on the cake. The absent father. Strike three.

I fought the legal system too. Through the mail I had a public defender and if you're not aware it is simply they are paid by the state the same state you're violating their laws.

I fell back to my roots religion. Dedication to this distraction was me grasping at straws. And it is said that it could take up to a year after consistent meth use to come back to the real world of reality.

I was suddenly surprised. Surprise slapped me in the face when I was handed mail from the deputy it was from my wife she went on to explain that thanked me for showing her what love is and how to give it it set Me reeling. Time dragged by not knowing how much time I was most likely going to do. More heavy on my mind when the rug is pulled out from under you; it isn't surprising that my attempt to keep some sanity I went back to my roots. Religion. That became my focus I started to memorize the verses. In the end it was quite trying on my emotions. I convinced myself that God was going to save me some from some trip back to prison. So when my parole was revoked, I had to face reality I was going to back to prison for at least a couple of years period.

While I was locked up quite a few came and went. Jail is often a revolving door.

When Pat came into the unit which housed 4 in total he confronted me asking if I was going to be going away for a long time period. I said yeah and unfortunately next question was do you want to get high? Without a second thought I answered yes.

Pat had come to bail out his friend who was in the jail. While the process took place it became evident that Pat was high. The deputy that handled the process called another officer and they preceded to allow Pat to go back to his car and when he attempted to leave he was pulled over. A search of the vehicle produced a tiny tin cap that have been used for drug use and contained a residue. Pat was arrested.

What the officer didn't know was that Pat crotched the drugs he had on his person before they arrest him. Pat had undetectably brought heroin and meth into the jail. Pat put a line of heroin and a line of meth on the middle of the bunk and invited me to snort these drugs. This would be a little relief from the future I was facing. It turned into a nightmare. Opiates can often mess up the physical aspects of the body. For me I was unable to urinate. Not really thinking this through I began to drink coffee and soda and Kool-Aid.

While I was doing this, Pat managed to bail himself out allowing him to regain his freedom.

I myself was in big trouble I could not urinate I tried everything from sitting on the toilet in attempts to calm down and pass urine. After that didn't work I went to a hot shower thinking that warm water would trick my body into cooperating. This didn't work either I had no choice but to inform the deputies of my predicament.

When the nurse came in after the deputies called her in from now it had become an emergency. I had drank so many fluids without relief my belly was three times its normal size. At the hospital they put in a catheter at the end of the hose there is a balloon but the bag began to fill the color was a chocolate brown. The doctor later informed me that I had very luckily my bladder hadn't burst the brown color was blood from stretching my bladder to the point of hazardous burst it fills multiple meter picture. The relief was more than words can describe.

When I got back to the jail Pat had been released. I was relieved of flying for he had left the tiny line of heroin for me. And after snorting it I nodded off for about two days. I woke up just in time to empty the bag of urine from the catheter which was still in me I hadn't been awake for 10 minutes and who walks into the cell block but Pat. He had failed a mandatory drug test which was the stipulation of his release. You guessed it he brought in some drugs.

Obviously not learning my lesson I snorted some meth as luck would have it the nurse came in to check on me also to take my blood pressure.

My blood pressure was through the roof she checked it several times and beyond my control and ambulance was summoned. Upon arriving at the hospital the doctor was prompted on getting to see me. His first words were why are you here? There's a cold stare that accompanied his direct attitude. I explained that the jail was concerned due to my blood pressure being elevated so high. He left without a word a moment later a nurse entered the room in her hand was a urine specimen cup. Now being that I had already cathorized all she did was drain some of my urine into that cup. She exited the room.

Within the hour the nurse came to see me with the syringe which she pressed into the solution dripping into my body. At this point my memory is quite fuzzy. I believe I took a nap. Before I knew what I was once again escorted out into the sheriff's car and taken back to the jail.

I was ushered into the receiving area and a deputy asked me where I got the drugs. "Matt we know someone gave them to you? you've been in this jail for two months. Where did you get them from?" The cat was out of the bag that urine test result must have been shared. Being shared with the nursing staff and relayed to the officers that I was high as a kite, whatever they gave me didn't bring me down I was ushered into a small holding cell when I refused to cooperate.

I was getting more distracted by the moment. I believe that obviously one's own life experiences contribute to one's hallucinations. Ones fears are also a major factor.

It is by bits and pieces that memory allows me to live through that experience.

I've always said I need to stop using that crystal for the gate it opens. This surely to me the minds gate the gate or reality and fantasy joy or mortal fear reign for real and hallucination are yet one. Being put in the small one man cell I tried to lay down covering my head with their coarse woolen blanket. It was through the separation of fibers that gate swung far from the depths of my mind.

There was an explosion in all I could do was lay and shock debris seemed to hold me down. I couldn't move there was a ringing in my ears that would surely have been from the explosion. It was in my mind I believed what must have what happened was that I had come together with my family and my dad and my mom were there.

They were there talking to me into my ear. It was I was told I was severely burned I heard from them talk. Talking around me about how badly hurt I was.

They told me I was in shock I was loved and we could finally leave this tragedy of this world I drifted away.

I don't know how much time it will lapse but I was awakened I was in jail in a cell.

I believe that a reality was not what it seemed my brother was outside the cell my much loved but deceased brother and come to the jail very much alive. I talked to him through the window of the door he began by telling me that it had been the plan for me to believe that he had died, he went on to explain it would seem that I needed tragedy to release myself from the grips of an addiction. He himself found himself losing a battle to these drugs and that is when the conspiracy began. It was a staged death he now lived in California; he drove truck and trailer across the United States.

I had a psychotic break the knowledge due to my drug use my life was to forever change. I could no longer discern reality from this drug induced psychotic break this strain was more than I could bear. How else can you explain a vision as real as the words on paper are to you and going to tune to a voice? It was my dad telling me Matt humanity died long ago we exist now that through a system of which you live much like a computer program life died except through a compilation of information we aren't enabled to experience these ends. After the terror have stopped, still far from the man whom i was when first arrested, my lawyer went on to reschedule my sentencing because I was in the thralls of a mental breakdown through drug ingestion.

Where else but in a secure jail cell. My ranting had brought a sense of pity from

my lawyer and I think jailers and judge and prosecutors alike saw me its impact on me I was sentenced to prison for five years and incarceration with five years' supervised release a consecutive sentence for an added two years totaling 7 year sentence.

I would never be again where the gate would swing wide.

I learned to keep away from

The Crystal Gate.

The End